BRAIN

Magona's Rise

Book 3

By Lucas Brady

Hardcover: 979-8-9867076-4-8
Paperback: 979-8-9867076-5-5

First paperback edition March 2023

Written by Lucas Brady
Edited by Lucas Brady
Cover photography Copyright © 2023 Lucas Brady

Printed by KDP Print in the USA

Kindle Direct Publishing
410 Terry Ave N
Seattle, WA 98109

This book tackles subject matter that may be sensitive to some readers. Topics include: depression, self-harm, descriptions of sexual abuse, talk of suicide, and disturbing imagery. Please continue with caution, and enjoy.

The books in the Magona's Rise trilogy:
Roan
Loca
Brain

~All available on Amazon.com~

This book is dedicated to life.
All parts of it; including Death.

TABLE OF CONTENTS

~The Messages~

"Do not read while driving."

-Brian Apostolico (The Eternal Brian)

"Meow."

-Rowan, Reese, Remus (Various)

"Despite the grim nature of Al-X's entire character, he was still one of my favorites to write. Up there with Death, definitely. Speaking of Death…writing about people dying is also super fun. That can't be used against me, can it?"

-Lucas Brady (Mic Braidee)

~The Graves~

"I wasn't expecting more visitors this soon."

"I won't be long."

Death kneels before an unfinished ring of five gravestones sticking out from the shining pink grass. The faint breeze juggles lavender leaves around the air, the trees losing the last of their foliage. The coldness of winter can already be felt, despite the heat of the shining yellow sun. Death slowly stands up, having to push against his knees to support himself.

He's aged, and the man beside him can tell. The man in question is Mic Braidee, the leader of the Valley Rangers and one of the last surviving beings on the planet of Valley. He wears a dark brown suit with two long coat tails fluttering in the wind. Golden buttons line the edge of the left side, and silver cuffs shine next to his veiny pale hands. Beneath the suit is a perfectly ironed yellow-white button-down shirt tucked into his dark brown dress pants. He walks toward one of the graves, hulking black boots crunching the fallen leaves.

"The Soldier...," Mic says. "He sounds like he would have fit in with the Valley Rangers, huh?"

"He fought valiantly against one of Magona's own men," Death responds. His bones shine a dirty yellow in the sun, and the wind flurries through the cracks that cover his body. Both of his eyes are decaying away and are surrounded by dark holes in his skull. He's ditched wearing any sort of rag and instead lets his rotting bones feel their last few breezes.

"K-T informed me of the whole Al-X situation. I'm also convinced that Magona has already taken over the CDD. Ty nor Uni have tried to contact me in weeks," Mic says. He bows over the grave marked 'The Soldier' and places a bony, six-fingered hand on top. "He'll have access to every Astrual Ring planet since the CDD already controls them all. Except us...for now."

Death doesn't say anything. He instead turns his corroding head toward the blocky, mountain-side stone base of the Rangers. The exorbitant amount of light from yellow and orange glowing lights around the corners rivals that of the sun. Death can see a figure watching from above through a wide window on the top of the base.

"So, who are these people? And why did you bury them here?" Mic asks.

"Depending on how fate sees it, either you'll get a visit from a woman with uneven skin or a peachy man with shredded fingers," Death begins.

"Ok?" Mic says.

"Either way, they'll need to see this. The woman must know about The Soldier...and the small print beneath the name."

Mic squints his eyes and steps closer to read the sentence beneath 'The Soldier.' He shakes his head as he thinks about the words.

8

"If it's not the woman…then the man will need to see all five of these stones to know the fight continued even while he was in stasis."

"The Seventh?" Mic asks. He turns his head to Death, who nods his head. Mic looks back at the grave and sighs. "Why'd you stick around for me to find you?"

"Mic," Death says, looking away from the base. A heavy breeze whisks between the two as they both lock eyes. "Your time is coming. I know that you're aware."

"I know that the next time you see me, I'll be gone," Mic responds. His cheerful demeanor grows melancholy. "And I've come to accept it. Allow me to die, and let me fizzle away. I wish not to live on afterward; it's too shitty of a thought."

"Mic, you could at least let me take your body somewhere," Death says. His crackling voice softens. Mic shakes his head and looks away.

"I have lived for countless years; seen plenty of loved ones pass. They treated life as a joke…as if they were partying until they were reborn as a new person," Mic starts. "But that's not what life is. You shouldn't avoid the necessary life only because you know something awaits you after death. That's why I don't even believe in your realm."

"Yet you speak of it as though it is real?" Death asks. "What's the explanation for that?"

"Just because I don't believe it doesn't mean it's not real. Hell, there are a lot of people here that don't believe in the seven gods, yet…here you are. Three left," Mic says. "Well, it was nice conversing with you once more."

"You have somewhere to be?" Death asks. Mic walks past Death, patting him on his bony shoulder. Death turns to face Mic as he steps upon a rickety dark brown wooden bridge, connecting the small island hill to an observation tower that overlooks the entire valley. The water below the bridge's supports splashes around as the wind picks up.

"Death," Mic says, stopping in the middle of the shaky bridge. He turns back to Death, who remains next to the mossy graves. "I think it's only fair to tell you what you don't want to think about."

"What's that?" Death asks.

"You haven't faded yet like the others have. It's the only reason they never visit me anymore, isn't it?" Mic asks. "They're all gone somehow?"

Death nods as he looks back to the stone base, which has dimmed in lighting along with the setting sun.

"So why haven't you?" Mic says. Before Death can respond, he turns and enters into a small bridge cross-section, where he disappears into the darkness. A sudden screech of thunder breaks through the cloudless sky; dark gray bundles of fluff appear from over the tall mountainous hills surrounding the valley's border. A view that reminds Death of time past.

—

Death was the first when the universe was created, not The Angelic. In order for The Angelic to exist, life would have to be made before him. And what is life without death? Death only appeared once he took the form of a human skeleton, which is now a grim reminder of the broken Earth II planet.

From the very beginning, Death was unbiased to everyone, for he knew that they would all be carried away to the same place in the end. There is no God; there is no Judge. There is only the ceasing of one's connection to their soul. Death knows this better than anyone.

When one dies, their soul is left unprotected, and Death makes sure to carry them into the Realm of Death, where the souls can stay pure and endlessly wander the white void forever. However, if the soul is not carried away, it will eventually disappear and be erased permanently.

The four dead Gods were not carried away because Death knew they could appear to him a limited amount of times. He mostly did it so The Star could spend his last moments with the one that tried to save him. And now, The Star, The TV, The Dog, and The Crusher's souls have all faded.

The Crusher was first; right after he died, he sat on the steps of his asylum until he faded into nothing. The Dog was next; he disappeared after appearing on Roan a few times too many. The TV was the second to last and was also right behind The Dog. He spent his final moments strolling through the ruins of Roan, wondering how he was coerced into believing an innocent soul like The Star was trying to kill him. And finally, The Star was the last to go.

While on the barbarian planet of Vhorlarx, Death found The Star pondering on a cliff overlooking a thrashing red ocean and a lavender-streaked sky. Death had not told The Star that he would disappear, fearing The Star would not want to appear if he was aware. So while The Star was already fading, Death laid it out to him. And before The Star was erased, he thanked Death for what happened on Earth II.

The guilt of not being able to save anyone nor being able to suffer the fate of death himself began to weigh Death down. And now, the only one close to Death left is Mic.

—

The Valley was one of the first planets to be created, a flourishing, green, and pink-heavy world with the first non-God creature, Mic Braidee. He grew close with six of the seven Gods, only fearing The Angelic as even from the start, the threat of Magona was imminent. Death treated the Gods as equals, the life within the universe as simply breathing time wasters, but was close with Mic.

They both saw eye to void-eye, both helping each other grow the Valley Rangers and Roan's economy. They grew close, almost too close at some points. "Jokes" of a relationship were tossed around by both parties, but it was unclear to both Death and Mic if they WERE jokes. Who knows, maybe they joined each other's side in another universe. But at the same time, it could've been Magona's start instead of The Seventh's cross-race relationship with a Kuroledy.

How ironic.

Despite being almost meant for each other, Death and Mic had one glaring difference. The way they perceived the straight line of life. Death knew what awaited beings on the other side, and he didn't bother to grow close to anyone after Mic since he thought of every other being as a dying breed.

Death wasn't a judge; he just was the bridge between the living and the dead. So why suffer the emotions of sadness after someone passes when it was known they would? No point in growing ties if eventually they'll just be shattered, right? And Death had one other factor that he had been trying to drown for centuries; he was the only being that couldn't be erased.

Death can't die. He didn't want to feel alone, so he didn't bother with relationships. And in the end, he feels alone anyways.

On the other hand, Mic didn't want to believe in anything after death. He just wanted to use the years he lived to do as much as possible for himself and others. All until he eventually keels over and dies. Why keep your emotions inside when the point is to express them? Growing ties to grow your self-esteem and personality is the point in life, right? To be as large as you can while raising others to that point?

And yes, the relationships and people you grew closest to dying are horrific to deal with, but that's what life is. Mic let the Valley be a safe haven for everyone, even The Angelic at one point. And they ended communications when Death found out about Mic's beliefs well into their ever-growing connection. Death wants to carry the soul of the only one he grew close to, but Mic just wants to be erased.

But will Death let that happen?

~The Cage~

"You're unconscious?" Death asks, wiping his cracked bony fingers along the outer edges of the crystallized lavender tunnel he finds himself in. It has an almost organic feel, with the coarse walls moving and squirming with a breathing-like pattern. Death wipes away some beige green liquid dripping from small, pore-like holes dotted around.

The floor Death walks across doesn't have the same feeling. Instead of an organic feel, the ground scrapes against Death's skeleton feet, and the brown, black, and white mixture match the appearance of decaying teeth. Matched with the dull aqua light emitting from the Vecimt planet's third moon outside, the tunnel reminds Death of the many mouths he'd seen mutilated in his time.

All the steps into the throat-like burrow lead to a dead end, where a featureless, colorless bundle of energy fills the empty space. Death knows exactly who-or what- he's talking to. An old friend, one that shares its mind and consciousness between a physical form and the clump of spirit it started out as. Whenever the visible body sleeps or is knocked out, it transfers to right where Death stands; the planet-or crystal formation-of Cöpar. Every few planet rings or so, a few crystallized developments are created, and sometimes it births life. And this life is a special one.

"What about it?" Death hears. The energy form of the ally cannot speak, but it radiates waves that can be interpreted as sound.

"Nothing, it's just this time feels different," Death responds. "Were you calling out to someone?"

"Yes, yes I was," the voice continues. "Did it redirect to you?"

"Depends on who you were expecting to hear it," Death says. He lowers his body and takes a seat on the rough ground. Since his conversation with Mic, which was moments after he was approached by Ty, time has taken its toll on Death. His yellowed bones are now reduced to sharp fragments, and his skull is more of a facade. The area around his brain chamber is gone; the eye cavities are like windows showing what's behind Death. His ribs are all gone, and his spine slightly trembles as it struggles to support the shattered collarbones.

"I wanted The Star to show up. There was a shooting star, and I think he would've loved to see it."

Death hears the waves, and he's brought back to a time when he sat next to The Star on the cliff sides of Jouruesa, located in the Churle ring. The view was beautiful...a setting purple sun painting glitter lavender against the snow-white sky. A thrashing red ocean spread into the horizon beyond the cliff's edge.

The Star lived his final moments as a fleeting soul next to Death, the only one that trusted and attempted to aid The Star during the dark times. Since The Star had his

16

soul exposed to the harmful energy of the universe, he was moments away from being erased forever. And he lived those last few minutes making sure Death knew everything was ok.

"Thank you for trying to save me on Earth II," The Star said. The line echoes through Death's missing mind as he remembers.

"I was only doing everyone a favor," Death responded.

"Even a small favor can mean everything," The Star said back. "Goodbye, and thank you."

Death remembers all the emotions he felt during the ordeal. Can I tell her about it? How will she feel?

"Meiv...," Death asks the bundle of energy. "The Star is dead."

While his sentence is met with silence, Death can feel the horrific emotions that Meiv emits. Sadness? Anger? No, the feelings she gives can't even be described. They can only be felt, and Death already wishes for the emotions to be gone. They hurt him, and he can't help but to wish he never told her.

"I am sorry about him," Death says. He feels the emotions settle, and the fiery response fizzles away. The energy of Meiv swirls around the fleshy purple room, whipping past Death and stopping at the entrance to the formation.

"Why can't you die, Death?" Meiv asks. "All of the other Gods can...but you can't."

"I have learned over the years that life and death coexist with each other. So as long as life exists in this universe, then I will too, despite my physical form being destroyed long ago," Death explains. "And vice versa. The universe ends if all of life is gone and I am killed. It's how everything works.

You know that my shadow has spoken to you before. I have come to accept it as the opposite of me; life. It represents life itself, and it's tethered to me just like the concepts themselves."

"Life... that's the seventh demiGod?" Meiv asks.

"Yes," Death responds. "Life is the shadow of me... but I am the shadow to it. So in a way, I am technically the seventh demiGod."

"Do you think what Magona is doing could kill you?" Meiv asks. Death is perplexed by the question, taking a few moments to stare past her into the outside starless black void of space.

"Magona is set to destroy all life and create his own. Wouldn't that bring upon its own Death with the creation of new life through energy? You're connected to the life created using the same energy as myself. If Magona recycles it... even if YOU aren't destroyed... then a new Death would be made... right?"

"The universe itself is life. So Magona could create his own life... but he couldn't make his own universe. Even the most powerful have limits," Death thinks. He focuses back on Meiv's energy form. "Everything, including Magona, would have to be erased in order for my shadow and I to rest."

"Do you have a plan for something like that?" Meiv asks. Death shakes his half-head.

"No…but if you stumble across any of the demiGods or The Seventh…bring them to Mic," Death responds. He walks through the bundle of energy, dispersing it all around him. "The Valley is the only beacon of hope left."

"You still want to protect Mic? Even after-"

"He still means something to me," Death cuts Meiv off. "There is still hope to save everything."

"You'll sacrifice your rest? I thought you knew that every being dies, no matter what," Meiv scoffs. "You're actually getting involved?"

Death doesn't answer. He walks out of the fleshy slit of the formation, fading into the void of space. Meiv's energy emits annoyance and evaporates as she transfers consciousness into her physical form. Death hopes he can undo what he believes he caused to happen. The imprisonment of The Seventh and the unleashing of Magona. Despite most saying that five of the seven Gods are dead, Death would argue six are. The Angelic is gone.

Only Magona remains.

~The Hunter~

Flakes of light gray whisk around the air from the dark, cloudless sky. Snow? No, the temperature is quite warm here. So what could it be? Ash, of course. From all that is left of the planet that The Angelic finds himself stationed on, waiting.

Magona stares out of a shattered clock face, out into the sepia and light gray scorched land. Branchless trees stick out from the dead grass, reflecting the utterly black view of space through the planet's cracked energy field. How did it get this way? Where exactly is he?

The clock tower that overlooks an empty valley continues to tick despite Magona standing amongst the broken rusty gears. The sounds echo through the quiet land, although Magona's deep breathing still remains the loudest. His body is adorned with purple robes with glittery golden seams around the edges.

His right sleeve has been trimmed shorter to allow the entirety of his bladed arm to shine in the fractured light of the ruptured Eternal Brain past the cloudless sky. The fleshy pink mound of land that sits in the middle of the universe shines brightly with heavenly white light beaming through cracks that have formed between the rose ridges and grooves.

"The Brain is cracking…and soon I will be able to enter and fulfill my plan," Magona says to Airn, who climbs up from the room below. Then, she jumps from the

20

open trapdoor onto the creaky wooden floor, dropping the scraps that she carries behind her. Finally, she places one of her white opera gloves onto his purple-clad shoulders, to which Magona turns his head around to face her.

"My Lord, I have swept through the base, including the underground tunnels and mines," she says, bowing before her Lord. The only thing she continues to hold is a sparking robotic head. "I even found a Leathean Machine among the wreckage."

She throws the head onto the ground, and it rolls to a shard of the wall casting a deep shadow over it. Magona looks down at the animalistic metal face, a lopsided rectangle with two splintered linen-colored horns on either side. A faded, painted-on grin reaches both sides of the face and ends at shattered cheeks that expose sparking black wires.

Above the mouth are two large red circles; one cracked and the other untouched. Six small, deep blue orbs dot around the larger circles, and only the three on its left side are ruptured, along with wires peaking out from behind. A small hole is left open at the top of the head, and the blinking red lights from inside shine out.

Magona looks at the head for a moment, then turns back to face Sergeant Airn. She now dons a welded-together T-shaped golden chest plate with an octagonal window in the middle. Behind the glass, a triangular orange light flickers from the lack of power. On Airn's legs, she still wears the same high leather black boots that have since been heavily sun-bleached. Her blood-red eyes that hide behind black streaks around her face avoid locking with Magona's ghastly bloodshot milky white eyes.

"I believe I have enough to bring my final creation to life. All of The Sacred beings I have made…they are all within my blade," Magona says, holding up his bladed arm next to Airn's head. "I only sent you out so I could complete the setup alone."

"So…where is he?" Airn asks, her voice trembling from fear. She knows precisely what Magona is planning to make…and she's afraid of what it can-or will-do. Magona lets out a hearty laugh after hearing Airn's shaking voice.

"The Hunter is in the deep reaches of the monster mine," Magona responds. He turns and looks out the ruined clock tower wall, into the distance past the dark brown observation tower and blazing stone base, all the way to a bundle of leafless black trees. They cover a small island near the vast dark blue ocean. The only connection to the mainland is from a small shiny red wooden bridge extending from the base of the observation tower.

"Why down there?" Airn asks. She walks past Magona and rests her hands on a raised, jagged piece of silver steel that wobbles with each soft kiss of the wind.

"He must be contained until we do the blood transfusion," Magona answers. "Hence, why I moved Al-X's body."

22

"Right," Airn says. She looks up into the sky where The Eternal Brain shines brightly with the cracks that have formed. She thinks to herself about what will happen when Magona enters the Brain…but even the act of thinking about it hurts. For a moment, she just wishes she could be free, but at this point, where would she retreat to? All that's left is The Valley and The Eternal Brain.

Now, they just await the appearance of the missing God: The Seventh.

As Airn daydreams for a new life, deep below the trunk-covered island, a blinding white facility rumbles as one of the rooms holds two glass capsules varying in size. One on the left of the room is about thirteen feet tall and is filled with neon green liquid. Floating around in it is the reconstructed body of Al-X; all his skin stretched over a dug-up skeleton from the graves of Zargo.

The right tube is about twenty-five feet tall and touches the very top of the room. It's filled with green goo, which covers a mysterious creature inside. The being remains still, unable to move at all. The glass around the tube is too thick for a laser to cut through.

The creature has a muscular build and is extremely large. Its skin is white, and exposed bone shines purple due to the top of the capsule's dull purple light shining down on it. Its right arm is shredded down to the shoulder, and the bone has been twisted into a blade-like apparatus, similar to Magona.

Its face is a mess of holes and stretched synthetic skin. Two large black cavities are home to Orugnic head-sized black eyes, and the skin around its mouth has been torn back to expose the coarse dark gums and dark yellow teeth. Over his body, thin pipes connect to his skin and wiggle to the top of the tube, where they bleed out and fasten to the multitude of mechanical boxes and servos around the room.

This room, and this entire underground lab, were all created for Mic to experiment and learn about life with The TV. Before the fall out of the Gods, that is. Hence, Magona knows about its existence since the entrance is hidden beneath a layer of false grass. Behind it is a white concrete staircase that leads down to the center of the planet, where the heat from the core was used to power everything.

After Magona's core-replacement plan went into effect and it was replaced with The Divine, the heat wasn't the same. So Mic had to improvise and pay Foremes to generate the energy for the planet. So he sectioned them in another lab room near the base of the staircase. It was a good, if flawed, plan that actually worked in Mic's favor. Even after the Foremes evaporated into dust after a few sun rotations in the Astrual Ring, the energy they created still lasted until The Valley went off course.

Off course through an invisible ergosphere around a forming black hole, one of many being created by the influx of energy in the universe. This caused The Valley to

24

travel lightyears all the way into the center of the universe, where the low levels of energy stopped the planet from moving. Now, it orbits The Eternal Brain. And as it does, two groups manage to find their way to it, both on accident and purpose. The first is a familiar group whose escape from The Valley proved to fail. They were lost in a wormhole wrapped around the planet, thus staying with it during the ergosphere's push. The second is two survivors that tried to flee to The Eternal Brain and wound up on The Valley.

Despite the coincidence of their arrival, Magona had been waiting for them. He knew they would come; it was just fate at this point. And it's also at a good time since The Hunter is done.

And The Hunter is hungry.

~The Tystarius~

"Wake the fuck up, man!" Lanzion yells in my face, holding onto my arm. Lanzion lets go, and my arm drops down to my side. I sporadically blink, violently thrashing my head around to examine my surroundings. I find myself back in the courtyard with the others and slowly retrieve my sense of feeling.

"You were in some sort of trance," he says. "But let's go; Brian scored an H19-Oral Bumfuzzle, and we're about to travel to Earth I."

"Ok, right, right," I say, looking back to the white stone wall, now a crackless barrier. What exactly did I just see?

"I asked him why he couldn't portal us there, and he said that would mess with his readings," Lanzion continues. "Anyway, let's go meet up with him."

"Right…right," I say, slowly walking forward, not taking my eyes off the wall. A quick image of the woman flashes in my head, but I blink it away. Who was that? Everything about the room seemed so familiar…have I been there before? Maybe.

"Oh," Lanzion says, stopping and turning to me. "Dharall is staying behind. It's his workplace, after all."

"Alright," I say back. The black sky and dark ground create a sense of claustrophobia; the blank white walls surrounding us feel like they are creeping closer. Well, maybe only to me; I do have a crack in my head, after all. Something about the wind strikes me as odd as well. It doesn't feel right, at least not for where we are.

One would think a planet covered in tar and black guck would have some heavy winds, but it feels soft. Soft like on a snowy planet full of little hopping bunnies, not a ship-filled fuel world. Does anyone else feel it, or is it just me?

I follow Lanzion through the courtyard into the blinding white maze that is the Stalis Station. Corridors and rooms filled with buzzing yellow lights, horrid smells, and filthy Pocomels walking about. Most wear dark blue jean overalls splattered with black and brown liquids, a few leather tool belts around the waist, and usually black steel boots. They aren't great for sneaking up on people.

We pass by a few talking to each other, and I recognize Dharall as one of them. I overhear the conversation, strolling as I pass. Dharall speaks of a fellow Hi-Tem Ring planet: Rhukers. I hear him explain to the others how a few of the native Trhools from the world fled to the Major Stalis Trade Depot, where they pleaded for help.

"They said someone was threatening the king," Dharall says. "An evil man…one with a large army."

Magona? No, how could it be him? He's gone. I made sure of it. There are plenty of corrupt leaders in the universe; I'm not going to stress over one threatening Rhukers. They're all unbalanced shitcakes, those Trhools. My thought train is interrupted as I blindly bump into the back of Lanzion. The heavy gray bodysuit he wears shifts on his body as he stumbles forward.

"Hey, watch it!" Lanzion yells, not turning to face me. I look past him to see a crowd of Pocomels gathered around the exit door, staring at some sort of white spotlight. I try to look over them, but some of their robotic legs use built-in springs to raise their bodies.

The noise from the crowd overwhelms my mind, and the volume keeps increasing as more Pocomels join in. They come in from behind and through the murky white walls' glass doors. I continue to try to look over them to address the situation, but as I begin to push through two scruffy Pocomels, a wave of sound blasts into the first line of the crowd. The heavy metallic legs and feet of the Pocomels crash against the floor, adding to the sound.

The screaming and craziness of the crowd begin to shake the building, and I hear glass shattering and bricks cracking as the Pocomels run amok. Their bodies are flattened, and they crash against the second line of Pocomels. I see Lanzion's large helmet a few feet before me, and he ducks down and pushes toward me. He slips in between some robotic legs, knocking into me as he runs on all fours into the hallway.

"EVERYONE, GET OUT OF HERE!" I hear Dharall yell from right behind me. I swiftly turn around to see him pulling running Pocomels and aiding them in retreating from the now uncovered double glass doors. The screams and crashes cover up the sound of another blast, this one shredding through the white paint of the walls. The wave also knocks some Pocomels over, their metal legs twisting and crushing from the force. I fall down as well, but my legs aren't metal. They're flesh.

My fall slams into the muddy, hard ground, and I can feel the crack in my head grow deeper. A sharp pain in my chest makes itself known, and I can luckily feel my left leg. My right, however, feels like every bone underneath my peach fleshy body has been ripped to shreds, and the skin around it pulses with intense heat. My purple eyes shine a deep lavender against the black floor as I shakingly push myself up.

I turn my body to lay on my back, attempting to hold myself up to analyze my leg. I try a few times to sit up, but my chest feels like it's being crushed from the inside every time I move. I huff and crash back onto the ground, holding only my head and right leg up as I see the damage.

The skin is bleeding profusely, with brown-red blood dripping down the wrinkles. The rotted brown and yellow bones peak through the skin, and they drip onto my chest. Seeing the horrid sight of a mangled leg with bones stretching through the skin in every direction leaves me speechless...and lightheaded. Each drop of blood echoes through my head, silencing the screams behind me. I slowly look up at the shattered double glass doors, everything blurring around me.

An intense, bright white light shines through the dense gray fog outside. A few moving shadows scamper around, hidden by the gray cloud. All the Pocomels that remain alive have already escaped, and those that couldn't lay dead before me. I lower my mutilated leg, the bones moving around my flesh as the skin touches the ground.

"READY!" I hear a creaky, distorted voice call out from beyond the fog. The spotlight moves around, like an eye looking for something to lock on. Despite the hazy feeling in my vision and head, I am still smart enough to try to escape. I turn back onto my stomach and reach both arms out in front of me. My bloody finger bones dig into the mounds of sludge on the ground, and I pull. Instead of pulling myself, my fingers drag the goo toward me.

"ATTEMPT THREE!" I hear the same voice from before yelling out.

"Shit…," I whisper to myself, unable to move. The feeling has completely gone from my right leg, which might seem reasonable, but I can't even move it. I can feel my body shake, but there's no breeze. Am I doing that subconsciously? I shouldn't worry about that right now.

"SEVENTH!" I hear from in front of me. I look up to see the Dharall running toward me from the darkened hallway. His metal feet stomp around the walls, the sounds echoing past me. He runs with so much force his legs indent the floor. "Stay on the ground!"

"Get away!" I try to scream, but my voice is silenced. As I realize he can't hear me, I can feel the presence of another being behind me. As I yell again, Dharall comes inches away from me as a third blast from the fog slices through the air. It reaches Dharall, and he stops in his tracks a mere three feet away from me.

"This is my land now. Trespassers will be eliminated," a voice says from above me. It's the same voice from before, the one that called 'ready.' Who is this man? And how is this his land? I look up at Dharall, who stands frozen; as if the blast paused time. His face is a shocked and horrified expression. "Are you still alive?"

He's speaking to ME. Have I really been able to act dead for that long? I thought my subtle head movements would've tipped him off. As I try to stay still like Dharall, I hear quiet yet noticeable footsteps on my right. They sound sludgy and oozy, squishing with each stomp. Without turning my head, I move my eyes to my right until they pulse with pain.

Brown, smudgy feet dripping with goo slowly cross into my vision. Each foot has several flabby toes, each throbbing as they scrunch onto the black floor. Around his bent, wet knees, the shredded end of a green scarf dangles in the soft Stalis wind. To my surprise, the man doesn't approach me but walks past. He stands before Dharall's frozen body, the muddy brown man holding his repulsively dripping hands behind his nauseous smelling back. His semi-quadrilateral head has a bundle of white sludge atop it, almost acting as hair.

He lays one of his hands on Dharall's left shoulder, his greasy dark blue muscle shirt staining with the brown of the man. I see the grip tighten, with the man's fingers angling inhumanly. They dig into Dharall's shoulder, glittery pink blood seeping from the wounds. Should I help Dharall? Is he DEAD?

Fuck it, I have a ship to catch.

"Excuse me," I say a little too loud. The man's flabby mud head spins toward me, and his body shortly follows. He rips his hand from Dharall's shoulder, and his body, still frozen, wobbles before falling backward. As the man walks toward me, Dharall's body crashes against the ground, and he shatters into little shards that slide across the murky floor. I did that. Was the man even going to kill Dharall, or was he trying to seed me out?

"Hello, you don't seem like you're from here. Usually, it's Pocomels after Pocomels, but you… you're different," the mud man says, placing both his vile toes in front of my eyes. I hold my head up, feeling the crack in my head splinter around inside my jagged mouth. The purple and lavender light from my eyes shines upon his dirt-brown body.

"Who are you? Who do you pray to?" I ask. An odd second question, but it can reveal any of Magona's surviving followers. The man doesn't answer; he just grabs onto my peach-colored shoulders and easily holds me up with no struggle. Despite my right leg being twisted a few moments ago, I find the feeling in it again and can move it.

I look down as the man lets go, and my metallic Pocomel legs level on the ground, holding me up. Wait, they're back to metal now…why were they flesh just minutes ago? Now is not the time to worry about that.

"I am Dr. Tystarius of the CDLO. Also known as the Central Department of Land Ownership. Formally known as the CDD," the man says. "Changed the name since some…twigs in the gears…decided to spread false rumors about what CDD stood for."

"You don't work for Magona?" I ask, in shock at both his answer and formality. Tystarius brushes off a few drops of black goo from his shoulders, and his featureless face ripples as he speaks. "Why are you attacking these people?"

"You see, we aim to control the rapid expansion of planetary ecosystems…and while in the past there was a meeting with Magona, we did not accept his deal," Tystarius responds. "But, you are simply a citizen and these company deals are to stay…confidential."

"Citizen? I'm-" I try to argue, but I'm cut off. Behind Tystarius' head, I see a glint of sky-blue light shining from beyond the dark hall. Tystarius must have noticed I averted my gaze because he turns to face the rising noise of slapping footsteps. The goopy brown body of Tystarius flushes into gray as the blue light molds into a familiar shape. A dangly, phallic blue object connected to two slim metallic teal legs, a forehead the size of a Formic skull, and blinking yellow eye lights that shine upon Tystarius' unmoving body.

"A goddamn Leathean Machine?" Tystarius finally spits out. He swiftly spins around, briefly looking at me before staring into the fog-covered land outside. As the footsteps grow closer, Tystarius holds one leg out behind him and crouches down.

"What are you doing?" I ask out. I stumble forward as I look over to the growing presence of 8088-Y running into the shattered white light.

"We have already driven fear into Stalis and its population. Leathean Machines are 'protectors' and are just a nuisance for the CDLO," Tystarius responds. "No need to argue with artificial intelligence."

With the answer, Tystarius pushes himself forward with his back foot, gliding through the air as he crashes through the already broken glass doors. He disappears into the fog as his legs pump onto the ground, the sounds of his steps fading along with his body. By the time 8088-Y finally slows down and stops right next to me, Tystarius and the fog are already gone.

"What happened?" I ask.

"The CDLO has taken over Stalis and they're already setting up Ether Guards a few miles North," 8088-Y answers. "We need to leave, NOW, if we hope to even make it off this place."

"Did Lanzion find you guys?" I ask as 8088-Y grabs onto one of my peachy arms. His metallic fingers

34

feel smooth against my slightly wrinkled skin. He pulls me along, almost dragging me across the sludgy ground away from the clear outside.

"Yes, and we're waiting for you in the courtyard," 8088-Y responds. As we turn the first of the many hallway corners, I look back to the double glass doors to see a black-haired woman peeking from the bent mullion. Have I seen her before? Yes, she was the one that I… can't remember…what was I thinking about?

I look back beyond 8088-Y's mechanical silver face, my eyes locking onto the blinding gold H19-Oral Bumfuzzle that hovers above the exposed courtyard. The walls I expected to see are now reduced to ash and rubble. The white color they used to have is now black and gray, little fires dotting the broken edges.

"What happened?" I ask as 8088-Y drags me to the H19. The ship has a triangular design and is longer than it is high. Two stubby wings extend from the front two sides, carrying several heavy-looking circular turbines. There are no windows on the outside, and the outer walls are coated in golden and purple gemstones. As we get closer, a light begins to shine from the backside.

"Those sound waves got harsher as they traveled. They built up until they clashed with the outside air of the courtyard. We were lucky enough to have been a few yards away, picking up Lanzion at Exit 7-bL," 8088-Y responds. He pulls me under the H19, and I look up to see exposed panels with wires and pipes flowing throughout. The white

35

light is slightly cut off as a mysterious platform lowers to the ground. 8088-Y aggressively pulls me in front of him and pushes me onto the ramp as it slams onto the ground.

"Quickly, go," he says. I scamper up the steep golden slope into the blinding light, where I come face to face with the group. Lanzion, who ditched his old outfit and now wears something new. Zarn, whose chiseled chest glitters in the white glow. And lastly, The Eternal Brian, with his red helmet and crinkly teal skin. A dirtied pink rag flows across his body, and his five arms cross.

"Ok people, let's get the fuck out of here," 8088-Y says as he pushes past me. He runs through the group and enters a dark room through a sliding pastel blue door. I hear the mechanical sound of the ramp rising behind me, and the slam causes me to jump. Brian quickly turns and walks on his triple-jointed legs into the same room 8088-Y is in.

"Where are we off to?" I ask. Zarn shakes his fluffy brown nest of hair and walks over to a leather purple two-seater couch next to the golden door. He plops down on it and closes his eyes. Lanzion takes a step to his left, blocking Zarn from my view. His outfit, as mentioned before, is different. He now wears a similar helmet to Brian's; a deep blue eye-covering mask with a yellow visor. On the side, there is an antenna identical to Brian's.

Gaping cuts and heavy bruises dot Lanzion's ashy skin, dirt and grime seeping from the wounds. His bulgy, uneven limbs hang as great sweat droplets flow smoothly down his skin. Seems like he ditched clothing altogether. How can I tell? I can see the slit between his legs extending up to his mid-chest hole. It drips with some sort of clear brown sludge and the fleshy pink split throbs along with Lanzion's breathing.

"Astrual Ring. Brian needs to search for it since we dragged him halfway across the universe into the Hi-Tem Ring," Lanzion responds in a raspy voice.

"What happened to you?" I can't help but ask. His dry, gray-lipped mouth lowers on both sides. I wait an elongated period, but he doesn't answer. He just stands in front of me awkwardly. "Hello?"

He ignores my questions and turns around. I get a 'good' look at his backside, the slit extending back to the bottom of his exposed yellow spine. Around the top of his legs, thin lines of muscle tissue and blood clumps hang around inside the meaty insides. How delightful.

I walk past the bizarre man through the rectangular pastel blue room. The area is featureless, besides the buzzing white ceiling lights and a shining purple couch that Zarn is sleeping on. The floor squeaks with every step I take and feels slightly moist. I stop in front of the mysterious door, seeing myself in the reflection.

My peachy skin glows in the light, both from the white and due to my lavender eyes shining out. The last remaining piece of my green shell dangles from my upper chest, and some dust falls off as I brush it. I don't even recognize myself anymore. That husk of green shit I wore was my identity, and now it's dangling from my peach skin. I look at my fingers, not by raising them, but by keeping them at my side and looking at the reflection.

The jagged edges of the skin giving way to the exposed skeletal fingers…the wounds and dried blood from the barbed wires…the skin that used to touch my Kuroledy is gone…and all that remains is the reminder that she is no more. I can almost remember how she looked…and how I felt around her.

Her beauty was unmatched, and her hair was like a cloud of black smoke…but it attracted me like a Zargon to a pile of meat. Her skin was smooth, and a hug from her felt like a million kisses. Her eyes…the color I cannot remember…but the feeling of looking into them and escaping to a metaphorical whole 'nother world…it was magical.

I can remember the last time I looked into her eyes…but the memory is a little faded. I know Magona was there…he struck her down. And I had to hold the Kuroledy I loved fade in my arms. I looked into those eyes…and knew I would never see her again. And that's the end of the memory. Needless to say, I understood the concept of death just as I do now. While I still retain the memories of the feelings I had for her, I knew she still had a time.'

Even if she was still taken early, I would have understood and moved on. I would have respected her in death as I did in life. But Magona did it; he meddled with mortal affairs. Something he knew I was against. HE took her from me. HE sliced the Rule of the Gods. HE was punished for it. And now, here I stand, thinking to myself about my hatred for him, despite banishing him long ago. Ever since I awoke, I have been alone for whatever ride I'm on now…and wherever it takes me, I'll go.

I have no point left in living. I wonder where all the other Gods are now…it might just be me left. I served my time and did my goals. I had found peace in myself mere seconds before I was sealed away forever. As long as Magona was gone. That's all I cared about. And now, I exist merely as a reminder of what-

"May I squeeze by?" Brian asks. I snap out of my trance to see The Eternal Brian standing in the doorway. How long have I been standing here for?

"Uh, y-yes, my bad," I say, leaning out of the way. Brian struts past, grabbing Lanzion's shoulder and pulling him to the chamber's far wall. I can hear them talking to each other; Brian seems stern while Lanzion leans against the wall like an annoyed child. I try to listen, but the sounds are too soft to be understood. Instead, I walk through the pastel blue door to be met with the dark yet lit cockpit.

"Hello, hello, hello!" 8088-Y's robotic voice cheers out. He spins around on a swiveling pole that connects to a little extension between his metal legs. Two flexible black tubes extend down from the ship's ceiling and slither into 8088-Y's robust faux ears. "Glad you made it on board. We were getting worried!"

"Where exactly are we going?" I ask 8088-Y. His jaw jolts down to answer the question, but we are interrupted as Brian reenters the room. He politely pushes past me and sits on an angled black leather chair. It shakes as he sits down.

"The Astrual Ring, my friend. I wasn't able to completely sweep it yet since I came to your aid. I noticed that despite you sending my sensors off the charts...," Brian says, holding two fingers up to his antenna. He clicks down on the base, and a green light emerges from his visor. A few inches before him hovers a vast hologram of the universe painted in a sparkly green shade. He zooms into the fourth ring, where the view of the Astrual Ring is enlarged.

"See right there?" he asks, pointing to some of the farther planets, the ones closer to the Churle Ring. "I've excavated all of those...and the energy levels grow with each planet. But when you were freed, my readings were COMPLETELY unstable."

"You wanted me to join you because you didn't want to mix up readings, right?" I ask. Brian hesitantly nods his head.

"At the time, yes," he responds. "But now I've been able to equalize your presence out of my system so that you blend in with everything else. But while doing that, the reading from beyond the stars have risen."

40

"I think it's some sort of energy harnessing pod that we could easily just…," 8088-Y says. He flips a few switches on an angled board above his head. He finishes his thought with a 'PLOOP' sound effect and mimics an explosion with his hands.

"It could be, but it's so odd. It's different amounts in different directions; I don't think it's one place," Brian says. "Needless to say, we are going to travel slowly once we get close enough, so you should probably get some rest. We'll stop at a recharge spot along the way…probably pick up some Shlurgers at Shlurghant Royalty."

"I could go for some pickled Zargon Shlurgers right about now," 8088-Y says, rubbing his metal stomach. Brian turns his head toward the hungry robot.

"Are you even capable of eating?" Brian asks. 8088-Y laughs as a smile grows across Brian's face. He quickly joins in the laughter as I smile behind them. Could I develop a new…group of sorts akin to the Gods I used to be a part of? They would be part of it, one hundred percent. Maybe not Zarn and Lanzion…I don't think they have what it takes. I should probably get some rest…despite having been IN rest for who knows how long. I need it, especially after the foggy confrontation with the mud man. I'll let these two laugh it out until they fall asleep.

I walk through the door into the empty room, looking around for possible living quarters. I can see Zarn across the room, looking out a steel-blue circular window out into space. What could he be looking at? Planets, maybe…or the stars. Probably something that makes him happy. Like how I can look at Brian and 8088-Y to have similar emotions.

A flash of bright yellow light fills the room, and I cover my eyes to avoid the pain. It lasts for a few seconds, despite feeling like forever. As I can sense the light fades, I slowly lower my arms to see Lanzion standing in its place, smoke emitting from in-between the lips around his slit. His expression initially seems confused, and he just stands in an A-pose, staring into space. I hesitate before taking a singular step forward, to which he jolts into reality and walks past me into the cockpit. As he passes, from the corner of my eye, I catch a glimpse of a little golden box.

"Do you feel?" Zarn asks from the window. I snap my gaze over to his as he stares out into space. I begin to step over to him.

"Yes, I feel," I respond. An odd question, but it passes. Zarn shakes his head.

"No, do you FEEL? As in, feel emotions through the air," Zarn says. "Anyone can just…feel things with their hands or emotions but looking at someone. But I seem to be the only one who can feel the universe. How it feels, and…how it reacts."

"Is it like a stimulant reaction?" I ask, looking over Zarn's shoulders out into the astral plain.

"I'm not sure what it is. Maybe I'm one with the energy? Either that or…," Zarn says. "Maybe it's just another personality laying dormant in the back of my mind. One whose feelings I'm sensing…but can't make out completely."

"I understand," I respond to him. I stare at the window, not through the glass, but at it. I see my reflection once more, thinking about what I've become. Look at me…a God in the past and now a walking reminder of the past.

Oh, shut up; it's not the time to think about that.

What? Did I hear someone? I quickly glance around the room, searching for the speaker, but only Zarn and I remain. Maybe I thought it up; it's possible with the leaking purple crack in my head.

"I'm getting a little tired," Zarn says. He finally turns away from the window and a swirl of light brown and mossy green flashes as he does. I seem to be the only one that saw it since Zarn isn't phased by the colors. "Do you have a Betferm?"

"Pardon?"

"A Betferm. I know Lanzion has one, and Brian probably does too, which means there's one left," Zarn answers. I tilt my head to the left, confused about what a…Betferm is. Zarn picks up on my expression.

"It's a device that brings you to a hole in-between time. Basically what lies inside a black hole," Zarn says. I tilt my head even more. "Ok, so sometimes a little crack in space forms, and it's dangerous. It can suck an entire universe through. Some SVE fields are built up around the crack in order to 'stabilize' the tear. A Betferm is able to pull us through invisible, air-traveling wormholes into the middle-ring of a black hole. There, we have bedding for sleep."

"Technology has advanced greatly," I say in awe. Zarn slowly nods, seeming a little hesitant. He walks past me into the cockpit, where I see the others standing around Brian through the door. Zarn crouches next to Brian, who's staring out of the holographic screen; the lights form an image of the outer planet that we grow closer to. Zarn whispers something into Brian's ear, but I'm unable to make it out. I direct my attention to the view of the planet, a blinding white planet with swirling teal colors flowing around the surface.

"Shlurgant Supreme," 8088-Y says, steadily picking himself off the sitting pole. He takes one step forward and rests his palms against the screen. "A harshly cold world with magma pits within the crust."

"Prepare to land," Brian says, patting Zarn on the shoulder as he grabs a yellow lever sticking out of the floor. Zarn turns around and jumps when he sees me, then slowly walks past me into the cabin. He only takes his gaze off me when the door slams shut. What is his deal? Maybe he is just a strange man...still, he needs to calm his oddness down.

Brian pushes the lever with three hands toward the screen, and the ship shakes. We're all thrown against the walls, all of us confused at the sudden crash. Brian is the first to pull himself up to his feet, his five arms efficiently supporting his weight. Still on the ground, I look over at his red mask staring at the view of Shlurgant Supreme. The problem is it's nothing but whiteness.

"What lever did you PUSH?" 8088-Y yells, clanking along the ground as he crawls to Brian. "The damn barrel-roll?"

"I've never flown a spacecraft before and the manual said-," Brian begins. 8088-Y grabs onto Brian's shoulder and hoists himself to his weighted feet.

"What manual?" 8088-Y interrupts. "For someone who was able to get us off Stalis pretty easily, I'd think you would know how to land!"

"Manual does say to push that," Lanzion says as he flips through a weld-bonded book of thick black Arachnavoid skin. On the outside, Stalinium letters are carved into the front cover, but I am unable to read them. 8088-Y turns, and one of his arms extends between my legs, and the squirming fingers latch onto the book.

"Give me this," 8088-Y demands, ripping the manual from Lanzion's ashy hands. His arm retracts, and as it slams back in place, 8088-Y stumbles to hold himself in place. He closes one eye, and the other twists forward from his face. He closely analyzes and inspects the skin-bound book, quickly flipping through the pages as if they were blank. Around the midway point, he slams a hand down which vibrates the pages. "It does say that, but you did it too early."

"Do I have to do it again?" Brian asks. He looks back at the screen, where the cloudy white fizzles away and a vast sea of thrashing teal water surrounded by an equal sea of snow-clad land. A shining black platform sits in the middle of the ocean, connected to the ground via four concrete bridges. We see a few other ships fly past us or away into the sky; models like the circular translucent red Ram-X-37, the rectangular transportation Lindest-eC-Straught, and even a light blue Hauling Ship model-P-o33 heavily hovers through the clouds.

"Seems we might be alright," 8088-Y says as we feel the ship level itself as it glides closer to the platform. I sense the temperature in the ship lower as the outside view is clouded with the sudden barrage of snow plowing against the screen. The sounds of the outside storm echo through the vessel as the engines die out and the ship rocks forward. For a moment, all of us are quiet until 8088-Y breaks the silence.

"We have landed."

"Time for some Shlurgers!" Brian exclaims, throwing his five hands up in happiness. The group all rush past me to the back of the ship, where the wall slowly opens and lowers onto the snow-covered platform. I wait for a few moments as I look back at the screen. The view of outside clutters up with white as the blizzard covers the external camera. For a split second, through the flurry of white, I catch a glimpse of a black-haired woman. She seems so familiar...but I can't quite remember her.

Although I have seen her before. She keeps popping up...have I recognized her before? All of those other times, I... can't...what? Was I talking to myself? I have to reach the others before I lose them.

The wind's noise is loud as it pulls me along its path. Stepping off the ship's ramp onto the ice-covered landing pad, the cold breeze hits me. It slams into my face, a frozen kiss from a snowy blizzard. The soft touch of the aggressively falling snow tickles my peach skin; the little flakes disappear against my body as I hold my hands up.

Snow was never something I had experience with...I mostly stuck to warmer planets closer to their sun. It's a nice feeling, all this cold. It makes me feel stiff and jittery, and I don't mind. I look up to the sky, seeing the cloudy white swirling around as the falling snow revolves around me. It has a beautiful look, with the weather bringing heavy fog and limited visibility. It's simply one of the many sights unbothered life can get.

Snapping back to the path ahead, I look to one of the four bridges extending to the mainlands to see the rest of my group waiting around. I walk across the structure, trembling in the coldness as Brian meets me in the middle. He has four of his arms crossed underneath a new, shiny pink cloth he wears around his neck and chest. Did he have time to clean his old one? Or did he just grab the new rag

47

on his way out? With the one arm that's not with the rest, Brian places it on my bony shoulder as his wrinkled chin contorts and resembles a smile.

"Glad you made it," he says. 8088-Y comes into view as he walks up behind Brian. His movements are obviously regular since he is unaffected by the cold. On the other hand, Brian shakes slightly as the snow brushes across his water-droplet-clad helmet. The antenna on the side of his head stands firm in the heavy winds, unlike his pink rags, which thrash around as the weather grows harsher. Lanzion stays behind near the visible fog line, but Zarn is nowhere to be seen.

"Do you know where we're going?" I ask. Brian quickly nods his head as 8088-Y stops behind him. "There doesn't seem to be anything closeby."

"Shlurgant Supreme is bare on the top layer of land, but civilizations have been accustomed to live underground. According to my internal brain chip, we are a few yards away from the closest entrance," 8088-Y explains. When he finishes speaking, he turns back and returns to Lanzion.

"I come here sometimes when it gets lonely or boring protecting The Eternal Brain…but I don't stay for long," Brian says. He looks behind him to the others, pauses, then turns back to me. "Just…if we get into trouble, let me do the talking."

I give him a confirmation nod as he pats me on my shoulder. We continue trekking through the heavy snow-covered bridge as it ramps down to the fluffy land. The mounds of white reach to about my knees, and Lanzion is almost waist-down in it. Every breeze worsens the cold, with the stinging ice mixing with the screaming wind. The blizzard thrashes and pounces at us as we trudge through the thick snow.

Throughout the walk, I notice the fog grows denser. At first, it was hard to see a few yards beyond, but now I can hardly see Brian, who leads the line. He has the most demanding job, pushing the snow away so we can quickly march through the violent storm. He really is the leader…and he deserves to be.

"We're almost there," 8088-Y yells through the wailing air. "Look out for a hatch on the ground!"

Almost a moment later, Brian stops before me. I grab onto one of his arms and hold myself steady as the wind picks up. All around me is nothing but white; snow on the ground, light gray fog, and the flakes that shoot down from the unseeable clouds. But, on the basis in front of us, a black square mechanical hatch peeks out from the white pillows of snow.

Brian kneels down and slides twenty-five fingers between the hatch's borders. He positions his feet to help him balance, then pulls the door up. He struggles at first, veins bulging through his skin and his body violently shaking. As the ice hidden within the hatch's insides cracks and we hear its sounds, he can quickly toss it aside. It lands on a fluff of snow, slamming right through it.

49

Beyond the hole that Brian just opened lies a dark hole and a rickety-looking wooden ladder.

"Shall we descend?" I ask.

"Gladly," Brian responds with a laugh. 8088-Y holds his arms out before us as we take one step forward.

"You need a light," 8088-Y says. Brian nods behind him. 8088-Y grabs onto his left pointer finger and snaps it backward. An inhumane crunch sound erupts from it, which causes Brain and I to cringe backward. 8088-Y's finger shines a bright blue, and he smiles at both of us as he spins around and lowers to the ladder. Brian and I follow behind, descending into the moist, claustrophobic hole into the underground tunnels of Shlurgant Supreme.

~The Stolen~

The caves were different from what I expected them to be.

For one, they are much more organized and lively than what I'm used to. And they're more square than circular. Plated with shiny silver sheets of metal, the walls of the Shlurgant caves almost glow with the lights radiating from green and purple flames burning atop black poles. Within the metal, sheets lie heavy industrial doors that lead to unknown areas. Carpets made from Zargon skin and held together using Arachnavoid webbing line the even ground.

The ladder ended at a fence gate; beaten Zargons hung from ropes around their necks hanging above. Some mutilated and unrecognizable. Other well-known Zargons that have been missing for years, according to Lanzion. Brian says it wasn't like this when he last came here and that something feels wrong. Lanzion and I dismiss the feeling just so we're not on edge.

However, I will admit that the aura I am sensing from just the entrance sight alone is off-putting. But that is what species do; they hunt the weaker prey, and even if we live in a more advanced society, that natural instinct will never cease. It is odd, however, that Zargons of all creatures were the ones hung here. They're supposed to be king of the food chain; at least, they were before I went into isolation. As we walk into the actual maze of tunnels past the gate, I notice something I somehow missed.

On a lavender and mossy Zargon hanging right above the gate, an incision carved into their exposed bare-bones chest. An elongated sword shape with an upside-down triangle overtop. Familiar? A little. I chalk it up as just the predator's symbol; to scare away anything in fear of being hunted. To let only the strongest and most willing enter into these caves of Shlurgant Supreme.

"How much longer until we get to the burgers?" Lanzion asks his voice trembling as we pass through the corridors of dead bodies and mangled corpses. Brian shrugs his shoulders as the dim green and purple lighting from wall-hung torches flares around us. Our footsteps echo around the curved ceiling, the only noise besides the crackling fire and distant cheering. Crunch, crunch, crunch, all along the path as our legs tire from the uneven dirt ground covered in mysterious white leaves.

"Here we are," Brian finally chirps. He stands proudly before a black industrial door planted in the flabby dirt wall. The cruddy metal sheets held together with poor weld-work give way as Brian knocks once. First, a woosh joins the plummet and is capped off with a bang as it smashes into the tiled floor on the other side. A wave of cyan light floods us as we lock eyes with rugged drunkards staring at us from beyond the doorway.

As Brian leads us into the tiled underground bar, groups of scarred, half-naked beings grunt and scowl. On either side, rows of contorted metal stools and hanging dark yellow tables line the dirty rose-colored brick walls. Curving around the room's far end, a crystallized amber high-top table is home to a displeased Formic. The Formic's appearance grows clearer as we pass through the eerie environment and past the glaring population. She slowly dries off a slender glass bottle with a flappy green rag.

A bubbly neon blue-gray face with patches of black hair around her baggy silver eyes. Hairy pincers around her fat-lipped mouth click as she speaks. A loose string of white cloth is wrapped around her luminous skin, from the bottom of her collarbones to the top of her pelvic region.

"You-*click*-paying-*click*-for-*click*-that?" she sternly asks in a deep, squeaky voice. She places the glass and rag onto the amber-colored table. A soft clink sound follows the action. Brian grows a cocky smile across his wrinkled teal face, sliding past me to grab one of the many misshapen high-top stools that line the counter. He plops down on a battered yellow-orange seat as we fill in the rest.

Lanzion takes a blackened amber chair, 8088-Y takes a sapphire blue, and I lean against a dark teal, opting not to sit. I want to be on the watch for anything out of the ordinary since this place doesn't seem like the relaxing area Brian was describing. For one, multi-colored flags hang down from the industrial pole-lined ceiling, all decorated with the same elongated sword shape with an upside-down triangle overtop.

Brian begins to speak with the Formic, but I tune them to the back of my head. I make sure to shoot my eyes all across the room, scanning for a possible threat. A brawl is the last thing I'd want to get myself into, but it may be necessary. As I stand, I begin to think about what I'm doing. Why am I here? Why was I freed NOW and not at any other point? Was anyone there to free me at all? I could be the only God left, for all I know.

Sometimes, it hurts to think like that. To have thoughts of the deaths of people so close to me. But that is life, being a living thing until death. Then, you're carried out to the Realm of Death…where I believe I will go after I die. Whenever that is. I try to shake up my mind by thinking of happiness; or what makes me warm inside. Thoughts of past events and what I could do now that I'm out of confinement.

I would be already on Roan, looking for the answers to everything. I need to remember all of my forgotten memories. Occasionally, I've noticed something will appear in my head, something I must have forgotten. It'll be without warning when I look at something specific. An image appeared when I looked at the heavy snow on the surface. A blur of a face with void-black hair…and a feeling filled my body. Happiness? Maybe…but it felt more like horror.

"Honey, you know why I'm here. We four request some Goddamn shlurger burgers!" Brian calls out from behind me. He throws all five of his arms up, cheering as Lanzion and 8088-Y join in. The problem is, sometimes, even the memories I do still retain are erased without reason. Something is wrong with me..., and I feel like my mind is splitting. Never mind the actual crack in my skull; I don't think that is what's causing it.

"Would you like it bulged or regular?" the Formic asks. That voice is triggering something...and I feel a rising sensation in my legs. Heat forms within me as the voice flows through the holes on either side of my head. I feel the world spin, and my vision wobbles in the corners of my eyes. I slowly turn back to the Formic, looking at her face as she stares at me.

"Hon? Bulged or regular?" she asks once more. The words deepen and warp as everything spins upside down. My head blanks, my legs give, and I crash onto the hard-tiled ground. The only feeling besides the heat in my chest I can feel is the crack in my head growing. My vision continues to blur as I see the Formic lean over the counter, looking down at me. Brian and 8088-Y both jump off their stools and slide next to me, Brian holding me up and 8088-Y holding my head straight up.

"Can you hear me?" Brian asks, but the voice doesn't match. Neither do the words. I heard the audio after his lips started moving, and it ended before he stopped. And the voice...it sounded feminine...and familiar. I blink a heavy blink, and everything ceases. The feelings fade, my vision restores, and my hearing is back. I suddenly feel myself breathing heavily as if I had been doing it the whole time.

"What did you say?" I ask Brian.

"I asked you what the hell was going on!" he yells out, his voice trembling as all hell. "You started to turn completely pale, and my readings went off the charts. It was like two of you suddenly appeared, and one just disappeared a second ago."

"I didn't hear your voice…or what you said," I say in quick breaths. I look around at the other creatures, all of them minding their own business. Were they watching until I looked at them? Or do they not care? Brian moves two of his arms over my chest and the other three behind me, slowly raising himself up and bringing me with him.

"Just breathe in and regain your balance," he says. I squiggle my legs around until the flats of my feet stabilize myself against the slightly uneven floor. I notice something as I gaze upon the three companions receiving their shlurger burgers from the Formic.

"This may be the effects still kicking me, but where is Zarn?" I ask.

"He's-," Brian begins, looking at both of his sides. "Wasn't he with us?"

"I don't think he actually followed us down here," 8088-Y chimes in. He takes hold of his soggy, bump-infested moldy green burger, squishing it across his face, unable to eat it. Pieces of red vegetation and droplets of saucy pink sludge smear all over his shiny yet snow-stained face.

"Did you say a name?" a crackling voice asks from beyond a dark, lightless booth. We all turn to face the ominous area, which is located to the left of the counter. I lean one of my arms against the countertop as I slowly walk toward where the voice echoes out from. I still feel slightly off put, with my spinning head starting to calm down. From the darkness, two red orbs fade into view. The light emitting from them is enough to illuminate the rest of its body, which is revealed as the creature steps into the room's natural glow.

I look up momentarily to see a large glass pane embedded in the ceiling, which I had somehow not noticed before. On the other side, an enormous hole reaches up to the surface, where snow is pulled around by the harsh wind. I can tell the sun is setting, and shades of orange cut through the white fog. It's a beautiful sight, and these colors are unlike anything I've seen before. All the sparkles and shades...I love it.

I turn my attention back to the monster from the darkness, which is revealed to be a blue-skinned Duhv with a blood-stained white glove hanging from between her legs. The rest of her rough, almost teal skin shines in the golden light as she hobbles her way forward. Her arms and legs are bent and contorted in a way where they can still function by helping her move, but they are definitely

57

not how they're supposed to be. Clearly, she's seen better days.

The front of her chest is gone, with the skin having been ripped from the bone, and her battered ribs can be seen poking through the shredded flaps of muscle left. Her deep red blood stains the surrounding skin, and lines of it streak down and conjoin above her black, bubbled, and charred vagina. The burns also continue down the insides of her legs, where they look as though someone cut the skin off and painted the torn skin with some charcoal.

"Excuse me?" I ask as she grows closer. I take a good look at her face, which is covered in rusty metal plates, clearly welded into his face. Skin bubbles around the edges and the holes above the eyes and mouth cast the facial features in heavy shadow. She looks like a monster. A metal-faced one that is.

"You were with him...one of you seems familiar. But only in scent," the woman growls. She violently sniffs the air around me, almost like a rabid animal. I slowly back away as her wild demeanor creeps us all out. Lanzion places a hand on my chest as he walks past.

"Listen here, bitch. I'd advise you to stand your ground and walk away," Lanzion demands. The woman, who's slightly bent over and still sniffing the air, slowly turns only her head to face Lanzion's direction. Lanzion continues to stand up straight, with his back perfectly straight. He holds his arms down by his side and closes his hands into fists. Without moving her bent body, the woman slides her arms onto Lanzion's, who doesn't move an inch.

"Pretty, pretty, pretty body. Smooth…like your friend," she snarls. "Maybe as tasty too?"

"Excuse me?" Lanzion yells out. His voice echoes through the room, and the woman lets out a blood-curdling scream as it does. My hands shoot up to my head, where I can feel my insides pulse from the sound waves. Who is this woman? And what happened to Zarn?

"YOU WILL FEED ME!" the woman yells. Her grip on Lanzion's arms tightens until his face immediately turns purple. She moans and screams as her arms pull apart and his rip apart. Lanzion's horrified cries mix with the woman's but are still not as loud. The blood spurts onto the floor, the woman's metal mask, and my face.

"GET OUT OF HERE!" Lanzion yells as he stumbles to turn around. He faces us, turning his back on the woman, and I feel 8088-Y grabbing onto my arm and pulling me as his feet clank against the ground. "GET TO THE SHIP!"

"Hold on!" I yell at 8088-Y as I quickly side-step alongside him. "Shouldn't we bring him too? We can fix him!"

"Fuck that, he's dead!" Brian yells, swiftly catching up to us. We enter the caves once more, where the once barren paths are now bustling with pale, slumped-over creatures blocking the way. The three of us brace ourselves as we burst through the crowd, the now red

59

lights of the cave blinking in and out as we pass by the people.

I'm almost out. I'm the first to make it to the other side, where the stench of molding meat almost knocks me out. What is that smell? I look around and find myself at the entrance to the cave, where the singular ladder is illuminated from the sky above. Snow droplets from the surface float down and rest against the rusting handles.

I look back at the crowd as it shuffles through the caves away from us. The occasional drip of liquid from the cavern ceiling is the only thing besides my own breathing I hear for a few moments. I wait in anticipation for someone to show up. Wait a minute…I hear something coming from the ladder.

The rough sounds of heavy metal boots clanking against the ladder's steps echo down, blocking out all other noises in my ears. I slowly turn back to the ladder, seeing a heavy shadow cast down to the ground. Who's that? There are other noises, too…sounding like a million engines coming and stopping at once.

I quickly look around for somewhere to hide because I have no idea who's coming down, and I don't know where the other two are. I find a small formation bolting out of the side of the cave wall, and I dive over and hold my back to the wall. The sounds of the boots cease as one loud bang reverbs through the cavernous paths. Can someone please make their way through that crowd already?

"There you are!" I hear 8088-Y yell from behind me. I turn my head to see 8088-Y standing in the wide open and Brian finally squeezing through the last few people. Do they not see the shadow on the ladder?

"Guys! Someones coming!" I try to whisper to them while pointing past the rock I'm behind. 8088-Y looks off past me to whoever came down the ladder. His mechanical body is cast in a dark shadow, and I can see Brian stop in his tracks. He slowly steps to the side, hiding behind a slight crevice in the wall. He looks over at me and puts a finger over his mouth.

The next thing I know, a bright orange light flashes through the halls, a loud bang blows through my ears, and 8088-Y's body is flung back. He crashes against the ground, and the man from the ladder walks into view.

~The Pull~

"How'd I run into your dogass again?" the man says. I look up from his square, black metal boots with spikes all around the bottom to see who the man is. His legs are covered in some wet, dark green fabric that crisscrosses all the way up to his waist, where it's held up by little shrapnel pieces sticking out of his body.

Over his chest a glossy yellow poncho hangs down over his shoulders. He wears a black helmet with a rectangular red visor and little purple markings on the side. His arms are bare and expose his bubbly, brown, dirt-like skin. As he steps into the red light of a fallen torch, a long silver rifle is illuminated in his hands. The end of the barrel is smoking, and he grabs onto the bottom of it and pumps a light brown choke. A small, ovicular mound of glowing blue matter pops out of the side of a small window on the rifle. It drops to the floor, where it lands without a sound.

I look over at 8088-Y. His body is laid out on the ground, with his arms and legs spread outward. Sparks fly out from the middle of his blown-open chest. Wires hang over the edges of his body, and the lights from his eyes fade out. The man stomps over to the corpse and lowers his rifle with one hand. He fires another shot, which splatters 8088-Y's mechanical brains out. They slide across the floor through the now empty caverns.

"Uni, I've found the caves," he says. "I have located a Leathean Machine, but that's all."

Who is he talking to? A weird static noise emits from the man, lasting only briefly. The man opens his visor, and a soft blue light from inside the helmet shines out. It displays a screen a foot away from his face, and a speaker icon is shown.

"I found out who he wants us to track down," a voice says from the display screen. An image pops up of the woman from before's mask, the one that killed Lanzion. Who is 'he' that they are talking about? Why are they hunting this woman?

"I'm about to seal the only entrance to this place so that she can't escape," the man says. He taps his helmet with his left hand and pushes it off. It crashes to the ground, right next to the blue matter from before. His head shines in the red light, and I recognize him.

He's Tystarius from Stalis. I really need to get out of here. I wait for him to walk a few feet away before peeking out from my little rock shield. I look at the ladder to freedom, hoping I can climb it before it's shut off.

"We need to go," Brian's voice calls out from behind me. I turn to face him as he slowly creeps alongside the wall to me, where we both crouch down and jog to the exit. "I am going to drop you off at my Eternal Brain so that your energy levels don't mess up my readings."

"Sounds good," I say, horrified at being in the open any longer. We pass some new Zargon corpses, probably what the smell from earlier was. They hang down from the curved ceiling of the moist cave walls, held up by their necks from black ropes dotted with droplets of blood. The color of the skin around their necks is mixed with the red and purple from the strings being tied so tightly. Where do they even kill these Zargons? And why put them here?

I grab onto the ladder first; my hands almost slipping as the snow from above rains heavier by the second. The pellets of white drop onto the handles as I hoist myself up, the drops landing softly on my face. It feels a bit cold, but the breeze that follows is excellent compared to the heat of the caves.

When I reach the top, I look around but can barely see anything due to the heavy blizzard fog. It's snowing WAY worse than before; I don't even remember what direction our ship is in.

"WHERE TO?" Brian yells out from the top of the ladder. I turn to him, or at least I hope I'm facing his direction, and try to see him through the white. It's so bad I have to squint my eyes, and they still burn as the wailing winds bash into my body.

"I CAN'T SEE YOU!" I yell back, holding my hands next to my mouth to hopefully carry my voice to him. The sound of an explosion from beyond the screaming blizzard makes me jump. What was that? I try to look around, but it's no use; the snow is too much. How am I supposed to get out of here?

"GET DOWN!" Brian yells as he appears from the solid-looking mist. He dives forward and wraps three arms around my body, and the other two he uses to provide weak support as we both crash to the cushiony yet brutally packed, snow-covered ground. "I CAN SEE HEAT SIGNATURES WITH MY VISOR! SOMEONE'S FLYING OUR WAY!"

As he finishes his sentence, I hear something in the back of my ears rise in volume. It sounds almost like a siren that slowly gets louder and faster with each beat. Could it be rescue people? Or could it be people hunting us down? Either way, I don't want to find out.

"DROP ANY WEAPONS YOU MAY BE HOLDING AND GET ON THE GROUND!" a loudspeaker chimes in, coming from the same direction as the siren-like noise. Brian looks up past me into the distance, where a spotlight switches on with a sudden thud sound. It lights up Brian's teal body, where he slowly raises all five arms up and uses his legs to get himself back to his feet.

"YOU TWO, FUCK FACE!" the speaker says as well.

"HE MEANS YOU!" Brian yells to me. I quickly roll onto my stomach, pushing myself up, joining Brian with my arms above my head. The spotlight grows closer as the shadow of something looms in the fog. The gloomy black shape lowers to the ground, where the light clicks off, and the sound of heavy boots follows after.

"I'll be rich once I turn you two in with the others," the boot man says. It's Tystarius, back from the caves. Dammit. I feel him poke his silver rifle into my back, where it dances around until he jams it straight through my spine, severing the control of my legs. I fall to the ground, helpless, as I watch him beat Brian senselessly with the same weapon.

It gets so bad Ty kneels down on the ground over Brian, continuing to raise and lower his rifle onto Brian's helmet. It shatters the visor, cracks the helmet's shell, and bends the antenna. All I can hear, besides the aggressive yelling of the wind, is the grunts of Ty, the sounds of metal hitting weaker metal, and the lifeless body of Brian flopping around with each hit.

After seemingly watching our kidnapping unfold in what feels like hours, Ty finally stands up and puts his own helmet back on. He lowers the visor and slides his rifle onto a little hook on his back. In his left hand, he tightly grips a few ropes that connect to a sizeable net-like bag, where the pale, soulless body of Lanzion is bent over backward around the headless, armless, and blood-soaked torso and legs of the woman from before. However, her mask is in the bag, latching onto a little stick poking through Lanzion's left knee.

Ty wraps his right arm around himself, latching it onto the ropes as well. He opens the bag up, where he grabs onto Brian's pink rag shirt and lifts him with no problem. Ty throws Brian's body into the bag, and it flops onto Lanzion's corpse. I'm next. He turns to me, where the soft layer of snow on his shoulders and striking helmet slowly melt away as an orange glow flows through his body, shining through the veins on his arms.

He places both of his feet in front of my head, which lays half-covered in snow. Bending down to try to be on my level while still towering over me, he places a muddy hand on my forehead. I feel my body heat up, from my head down to my waist. At first, it's nice since the snow, breeze, and blizzard aren't exactly warm. But soon enough, after a few seconds, it hurts.

I feel the muscles in my upper body cramp and tighten, and sweat drops from my forehead. My body begins shaking as I struggle to even move my left arm, as the muscles are too tense to flex around. I feel my vision fading as well, the heat becoming too much. I can't do anything…I can't save myself.

"Go to sleep, and you'll wake up in a better home. With Mag-"

I'm unable to hear him finish his sentence. I just black out.

—

"Two dead, one alive, and one in serious condition," a voice says, squeaky and fast. "How did you manage this? I sent you for one, and you come back with four?"

"I got the target killed," Ty's voice cuts in. "I picked up some souvenirs for Magona."

What? My eyes shoot open. The light burns them, but I don't bother looking away. I find myself captive with golden chains to a cushioned gray couch, with Brian on my left and the woman's body on my right. Her head is gone, and the neck is split open from where the rifle bullet went through. Blood and little pieces of flesh and muscle hang down her body, covering her upper chest in gore.

On the other hand, Brian is very much alive but critically injured. He turns his head to me, and his visor is completely shattered. His eyelids droop as blood trickles down from wounds, slits formed from the broken green glass of the visor. Though heavily shadowed, I can see his eyes; cloudy purple orbs with a spinning black circle in the middle.

"Are you ok? Are you alive?" I ask Brian frantically. He just slowly shuts his eyes and turns his head down to the green-stained floor covered in light brown mats. I hear a soft sigh come from Brian as he arches his back forward and heads down, presumably sleeping. On my left, past him, is a gray wall dotted with little white papers. Each one has a photo, a price tag of their respective species' currency, and a name.

I'm with bounty hunters. But they seem too formal.

Right across from my person is about two feet of walk space, then another row of cushions. On my right, past the woman's corpse, is a small, circular window that's currently frosted over with some sort of orange frost. Rustling can be heard from the other side.

There has to be a way to escape. Right? I can't worry about anyone besides myself, but I'm only cuffed by my arms. Maybe if I…try to kick something…with my legs. I start to scoot forward, attempting to kick my legs before I remember that I can't; I can't control them anymore. What am I going to do?

Something opens to my right, and my head shoots over to see that the circular window wall is a sliding door, and Tystarius stands in the frame. His tall, broad demeanor and now all-black outfit cast a heavy shadow onto our tiny cabin. He takes a few steps forward, letting the door close behind him.

The light from the window fades as a small shield slides down overtop it. The room goes black. A small click and a hiss flow into my ears as a teeny-tiny flame ignites in the middle of the room. The dark helmet of Tystarius reflects the orange light as he raises his visor. He raises the flame up to his face, where his actual FACE is visible from the light.

He raises his other hand and slowly wipes the brown smudge off his head, revealing the proper body form of a Dierariun face. Beneath all the helmet and all of that slocky grossness is a gray orb with a green, broad, thin-lipped mouth above one unevenly placed eye. The ring around the pupil is a smokey, milky yellowish color that matches the poncho he had on earlier. His skin pulses with rhythmic white lines.

69

"You mentioned Magona," I say to him. A smile grows upon his face as his charred, black, and yellow teeth show themselves. He lets out a hearty laugh, putting one hand on his stomach.

"He will love to see you," Tystarius laughs. "I know who you are. You are The Seventh… I'm not sure how I didn't pick up on it as a child. I grew up Sevrinchístt with my parents, and I know about you all. It was…special to meet one of my heroes, but…I work for him out of fear."

"He is dead. You are aiming for a goal that doesn't exist," I say back. I feel my headache crack, my face warming up as a voice tries to speak to me. 'You,' I think I hear it say. Tystarius leans closer to me, placing one hand on my left shoulder.

"Dead? Like how you left him?" he growls. "He is very much alive."

"What?" I yell out. He can't be serious; I banished Magona! The Angelic is dead! HE SHOULD BE! He's lying; he has to be. I try to make sense of the situation, but it overwhelms me. I start to have trouble breathing as my lungs seemingly give out. I was imprisoned for erasing Magona…and he's BACK?

"We here at the CDLO are glad to work under such a superior being. He'll certainly be happy to see you. Get comfortable. We'll be arriving shortly."

~The Brain~

Space is so beautiful. Just a collection of burning stars and colorful planets surrounded by darkness. Some can compare their lives to space. Can I? I'm not sure. I used to have that 'color' within me; the love for my mortal. I don't remember much about her...but at the same time, I do. All my memories are foggy. Sometimes I remember them...sometimes I don't. It all depends on the situation. I'm being reminded of the hell I went through that day.

"Nobody will believe you," he said to me. Magona...not The Angelic. Magona had already taken over by that point. I was holding my Kuroledy in my arms...watching as her body faded away before me. Her limbs shriveled to dust as I screamed. I screamed Magona's name. The only person I could focus on at that moment was him.

My screams echoed off the sand-colored brick chamber, as did the clang of Magona's sword onto the ground. His electric glowing orange sword provided most of the light in the room beside a few small white torches. He had his back turned to me. I dove forward and grabbed the handle of that sword...and my mind was cloudy. Hate clouded my judgment.

Hate...fear...and a feeling of betrayal overpowered my better self. I couldn't help what I did next. I flung that sword through the back of Magona's knees. From the wounds, his body crumbles into the same transparent dust that my Kuroledy disappeared into. What have I done? He was right. Nobody will believe me.

And nobody did.

I was sealed away and kept in The Crusher's mansion. He kept me as a trophy and a reminder. A reminder that no matter what, all of us Gods are equal in strength. Even if we don't see that. Why me? Why was I the one to be thrown into the mix? I wasn't doing anything wrong.

Was I?

"Shouldn't we have arrived by now?" I hear Tystarius yell from the other side of the window wall. "Why did you think a shortcut through a Duration Maelstrom was a good idea? We might be there quicker, but to him, it'll be FOREVER!"

"Sir, I didn't choose to go through one. It just appeared before you walked back here," a different voice says. I look at Brian, who is staring with wide eyes at the frosted window. I look back as the wall opens, and Ty storms in with his helmet on. I brace myself for anything, but he walks right past us.

I watch Tystarius slam both of his muddy hands onto the wall opposite the cabin's door, cracking parts of the concrete as he grows his aggression. I look back to Brian, who finally turns toward me. Brian doesn't seem phased; he just keeps his head down and his eyes closed. I can barely see his eyes as he carefully slips one of his arms free from the binds behind him.

"What are you doing?" I quietly ask, leaning over to him so Tystarius cannot hear. He points his now-free hand over to Ty, whose cracked wall now leaks sky-blue light into the gray-washed space.

"He's distracted," Brian responds. "I'm using this chance."

"IF YOU'RE THE REASON WE ARE LATE, I AM GOING TO KILL YOU!" Ty yells, the highly blunt bangs coming from his fists as they pound the wall echoing between each word. Splotches of brown and dark yellow goo squirt around Ty, flinging off his body as he beats the wall. "I WILL JUMP OUT OF THIS MAELSTROM MYSELF AND DELIVER HIM THE-"

———

"Come on. Wake up."

I open my eyes to see Brian standing over me. His helmet is covered in ash, and heavily torn cuts slash across his skin, leaking rainbow fluids. He scarily looks around as if waiting for someone to jump at him. What happened? Did I pass out?

"What happened?" I make out, my words slurred and slow. Brian grabs onto my right arm with all five of his, pulling me up onto my feet, to which I stumble to catch my balance. I notice the floor is exceptionally slanted, and I have to angle my feet just to stand straight. The back wall of the ship is wholly shattered open, and a dark, foreboding light shines upon us. I look out to see a trench in the scorched sepia and light gray dirt leading all the way to our vessel.

The view of the blank, colorless sky reflects the deceased feel the land around me has. On either side of the channel, black, branchless trees tower over the fields of dead grass. A ticking sound echoes through, shaking some of the thinnest branches and skinniest blades of grass still remaining. Brian steps out from the ship, over some green flaming debris, out onto the mushy dirt path. He looks up to the sky just out of my view, where the color of his skin fades.

Tick.

"No," is all Brian lets out as he falls to his knees, the sound oddly crunching as it smacks against the ground. I quickly jump over the woman's corpse from before, which now finds itself spilling guts onto the ship's deck and out onto the earth to join Brian in looking toward the sky. Towering over the planet and consuming all of the remaining rouge light from space is a mound of pink, fleshy material that begins to crack all around with white light shining through.

Tick.

"What is that?" I ask.

Tick.

"My home. We crashed here…wherever we are…and my readings were off the charts when I awoke," Brian says. "And I know why."

Tick.

"Brian. What's going on?" I ask, desperate for answers. Around us, little gray pellets fall to the ground. Snow? No, the land is too harsh for such a pretty sight. Ash is more like it. "What is that pink brain thing?"

Tick.

"That's my home," he says, his voice gone and his spirit diminished. He's heartbroken? Maybe devastated is a better word. "I was made to watch over this universe, and all others. To make sure the energy level of each one was at a balance with all the others."

Tick.

"But, one day, I went out to look for a heavy reading on my scanner. Which when I met you," Brian continues. He rests his joints, letting himself flow onto the ground, where he bows down to his brain-like planet. "We went through a Duration Maelstrom, which sent us forward in time. And now we're too late. We can't stop the cracking from happening, and that brain is a hub to all other realities."

Tick.

"Everything and everyone in every universe and reality will perish if that is destroyed. It's not an erase, either. The universe won't pop out of existence. It will send a shockwave first, killing all remaining life by incinerating their bodies. Then it will pull the Cosmo Field toward it, swallowing everything else whole."

Tick.

"What are we going to do?" I ask. Is this the end? I've come this far…and I die here? Like this? Ever since I was freed from that prison… I've been dragged along on this journey. And now-

Tick.

"We are all meant to achieve one great thing in life," a feminine voice calls out. Hm? Who said that? I look around the area, not seeing a single another living soul. Just the dark, haunting reminder of a thriving planet torn to its core from whatever event we passed in time.

Tick.

"I'm going to wait here," Brian says. "Go on your way. I brought you here, and I wish to be left alone now. Death is peaceful once you welcome him. I should have stayed on my brain."

Tick.

"I forgive you," I say. Was he asking for forgiveness? Probably not, but everyone's soul should be at peace before they die. A clean soul is a happy afterlife. I begin to walk away from him, passing by the crashed ship. It's a light gray box with a small window on the front, where I can see a mess of colors in the front seat. Its head is smashed against a makeshift dashboard, with broken shards of the window's glass lodged in his forehead.

Tick.

"All the events that have transpired within the time since you had awoken have been for a reason," the woman's voice from before calls out again. It sounds echoey and distant, yet familiar and close simultaneously. "You are meant for something. You just have to find it."

Tick.

Wait. I know that voice.

Tick.

"You just have to find it."

Tick.

Kuroledy.

Tick.

I turn around to see a woman standing amongst the planet's darkness. Her figure seems to glow despite emitting from her body. She doesn't even seem to be physically there…like my body is projecting her. I steadily reach one of my hands up to the crack in my head, where I feel some sort of heat discharging from it. My fingers follow the heat source until I can't move them any farther, and they point toward the woman.

Tick.

Pale, bone-colored skin pops from underneath a heavy amount of black hair, which ends around her waist. The rest of her body is decorated in a baggy, void-black one-piece that covers all of the skin except her hands and from the neck up. Her legs are crisscrossed with each other, and they're adorned with knee-high black boots. Her face is blurry, and I try to squint to see her features, but to no luck.

Tick.

"You know me," she says.

Tick.

"I want to," I say back.

Tick.

"I've always been with you. I'm the reason you've been having head pains," she laughs. The blurriness of her face begins to come together to form something familiar as I remember everything.

Tick.

"Grys?" I say. She nods as her face becomes clear.

Tick.

Emerald green eyes. A soft, round face. A big, but cute, nose. Thin eyebrows that curve on either end. Heavy eye shadow. I've been getting flashes of her... she's been attempting to communicate with me.

Tick.

"You've been with me this whole time?"

Tick.

"I didn't know when to show myself. But knowing the situation here... it's a good time. A soul must be at peace before it carries on," she says.

Tick.

"Am I at peace?"

Tick.

"You will be."

Tick.

Before I can say another word, she begins to fade. No, I need her. She can't go this soon. I just got her back. Please don't let this be it; I'm about to die. Can't she stick around for longer? I watch as she smiles, the same one I used to see.

Tick.

"Are you leaving me?" I ask.

Tick.

"I only have a limited amount of time to talk to you," she explains. "I've wasted so much already…I would sit by your imprisoned self hoping someone would set you free."

Tick.

"This is it?"

Tick.

"There's always the afterlife. I still haven't been," she laughs. I love her laugh. I've missed it, even without knowing,

Tick.

"I'll miss you," I say, as the only part of her left is her head.

Tick.

"You won't feel that for long," she says. Her smile is the next to fade as she says one more thing. "Missing is how you feel before you see someone again. Because of that, it always guarantees you will see them again."

Tick.

"I'll still miss you," I say as she disappears, and I feel the skin around the crack in my head stretch together, sealing away the tear. The heat swiftly turns into a cold feeling as a breeze rips through the air. I feel empty.

Tick.

She waited all this time…just for that? I don't feel at peace. But…it was nice to see her again.

I wait for another ticking noise, but it doesn't come. I look up at the brain, which is much closer than before. The cracks are more significant, too, with the light actually beginning to shine down on the planet. Was that all in my head too?

"Excuse me? You look very familiar," a girl whispers from behind me. I turn to see a pale, white-skinned woman with long black hair and-

"Seventh?" a man's voice from behind the girl cuts through my thoughts. Looking over, I see a tall, well-mannered man standing over the black-haired girl. He dons a wrinkled, hole-ridden dark brown collared suit. On his face, a pair of shattered red-rimmed glasses hang awkwardly over his large, chiseled nose. Mic Braidee…another person I haven't seen in…a long time. Hating to ruin the reunion, I say one thing to break the silence.

"We're all going to die soon."

~The Water~

"Are you feeling better?"

Not really, I want to say, but I can't.

"Yes."

My stomach still feels like it's in knots, and my head is spinning faster than before. I haven't eaten anything in a few days; I've been too busy. We had just stopped at a learning center, and I 'borrowed' some books about after-death concepts, soul planes, and reanimation. Hopefully, they don't need the books anytime soon.

I need them to research if I can bring 'him,'...REEZ...back. I need him right now...he would know what to do. I can feel the threat of Magona creeping closer. All the planets we've traveled to so far have warned us of his presence. They know he's coming, just not when. If I had Reez...I would feel safe. I would feel protected. I would feel-

"JANX!"

"What?" I yell back, spinning around to see Imbue's yellow-tinted skin and green leather overalls. He steps into the room, his piss-yellow boots stomping with each step. He passes through the open entryway, the scent of smoke flowing in from behind him. The dim white light emitting from a singular hanging bulb above us flickers with each boom from Imbue.

He walks over to the far wall, where he crosses his arms and leans on the many shelving units dotted across.

He turns his head to look at one of the shelves, one holding a few canisters of multi-colored blood from creatures I have slain traveling with Imbue. Alongside the vials, Reez's weathered brown leather notebook collects yellow dust. Imbue walks over and picks it up, blowing the dust off. It flies in the air and disappears after a second.

"Dust this fast? It hasn't been that long since you first boarded this ship," Imbue says. He sticks his thumbs into the middle of the pages, carefully splitting the journal open to the beginning of the blank pages. "Do you know why he never finished this?"

"He was killed," I feel as if I am forced to say. "I already told you."

"I know, but this page isn't done. Neither of them are," Imbue says. I reluctantly turn to face him as he holds the book out, and I look upon the last two pages with any writing. "Would you like me to leave you alone? I just came in to see what you were doing."

"Where are we heading now? I can't remember, my head is spinning a little," I ask him, ignoring his question. His expression shifts into an almost annoyed look as he crosses his arms and leans to his left.

"I've told you a million times, Janx, we're off to Secula in the Mesial Ring," Imbue says, trying his hardest to sound nice about it. It's true; he has told me a million (and one) times. "You can stay here if you'd like. I just need to drop off an order and run some errands. You know where to find me."

As he leaves the room, he pats his left shoulder, where a small black box is clipped onto his body. A make-shift walkie-talkie, if you will. I have one too, which is stuffed in one of my inside jacket pockets. I give him an affirmative nod as I turn around and put my face into the pages of the journal.

There are a few pages I reread from time to time. Especially since there really isn't anything else to do. It's just… I've learned so much more about Reez than I ever knew. Some of it…I don't know how to describe it. I can feel the emotions that he went through while writing. And it's what the majority of this journal is; his suffering and early death. I flip back to page three. Starting from the top, I reread his story. The only way to pass the time, it seems.

ENTRY 2

'Hello.

My name is Reez, or at least, that's how I know myself. This is only my second entry, and I come to it with…things. Good things? Maybe. I'm off on a work mission for my boss, and I don't know…everything feels off. I'm questioning my life right now. And who/what I am. I don't even know if I want to be alive right now. I'd be too lazy to harm myself, anyway.

I need to think positive thoughts. It's only two weeks out here; I can manage. Maybe it's the loneliness getting to my head? Whatever…I can manage. I think…if I had someone to talk to…it would all be better. I'd be more

83

mentally stable than I am now. I have problems. I know I do.

But we all have problems. So I'm normal.

I think that's all…until next time?

-Reez'

A short entry, yes, but the first one was much more upbeat. He had been so excited to start this journal, talking about how he was getting more time off other projects in order to really dive into his work. At this time, I wasn't even born yet. Dismissing my thoughts, I turn the page to read the next entry.

ENTRY 3

'Happiness is found when you need it the most.

I found a woman today…a human one. With the most beautiful black hair…and a cute, pinchable face with the most perfect lips. Her eyes sparkle of green light and they honestly complete me. She's everything I need; a makeshift therapist, a best friend, and a possible lover??? Ooooooo…I can just imagine what we could be.

We met at the local freshwater source that I frequent around this time. She approached me just like an angel. I think the sun was even shining on her too…and I love it. I love her.

I love her.

I love her.

I love her.

I get to see her tomorrow. I may forget to write in this journal for a bit!!! Let's see how it goes! Until next time!

-Reez'

Part of the yellowed page is dotted with little smiley faces and doodles of faces. I believe it's depicting the face of the girl...with long, wavy black hair, emerald green eyes, and a round shape. She's pretty. But...I can't say that knowing what happens. I quickly look up from the book, to a small tablet on the wall, showing a pixelated view of outside. I can barely see the approaching planet, so I have time.

ENTRY 5

'Am I normal? I don't really know.

I was at her house...a small, lovely cottage off the coast where it was just us two. She had a pie cooking in the oven, and I could just smell the fruity scent traveling through the air as we laughed on her leathery couch. Between laughter, she would always give me some look...and I still don't really know what emotion it was.

But anyway, the night went really well...for the most part. At some point, we started playing some childish games. Shit that I used to play when I was in learning rooms back as a wee lad. But...she started asking risqué questions. Randomly, too. I've never really been in any sexual situations or conversations, so I didn't really know how to react.

I don't know much about this stuff. My parents, rest their souls, weren't very vocal about it. I know the basics, but it all seems...gross? Am I supposed to enjoy having my genitals inside someone else for purposes other than reproduction? Can I not just...be with someone for their heart? Their spirit? Their person?

Who knows.

Kind of a bummer, but hopefully it gets better. Till next time.

-Reez'

I flip a few pages. Why do I reread all this? All this...trauma? It seems personal like I shouldn't be seeing it. Sometimes...you can't believe something. Or that you see someone else differently...and that's what happens when I read these entries. I see someone who I love and care for...someone who I need and who needs me. Someone who was mentally wounded by events that I wish I could've been there to stop.

What I still can't understand is...how could someone so happy have so much emotional baggage? I made him feel so much better when he was with me. He's always on my mind. I miss him. I guess I read this book repeatedly because...just seeing his handwriting makes me want him again. And reading these words and emotions…makes me want to help him. Anyways, I continue to read on.

ENTRY 11

'I'm a very relaxed, no-fucks given person.

I think that's a bad thing. I don't know when to really say 'no.' She's been touching me for a few days now…and I don't really know how to feel about it. I guess she thinks my body is just that good? I've just never really felt confident about the places she's touching. But if she likes them, it must be good.

I was back at her house, it's the only place it happens. This IS my first relationship after all, so I'm getting used to it all. I'm just uncomfortable about it all at the moment, so I'll hopefully be just like her soon enough. She's making me try a lot of weird stuff…like touching myself to thoughts of her. I haven't done it yet, I just lie to her that I do. She said it's something normal…and that it's odd I don't do it. Do I look like the kind of guy to touch myself? I feel weird just washing it in the morning.

Whatever. She's my girlfriend now and I love her, so I'll listen to her. Until…next time.

-Reez'

Next page.

ENTRY 12

'It's becoming a more occurring thing now. And I guess I like it. Still a little uncomfortable with it all…her touching me and all.

What's annoying is that…I can't touch her back. Shouldn't relationships be equal?

She made me touch myself again. Almost forced me too…pleaded and everything. So I did. I locked myself in another room and did it…to nothing. It kind of hurt, to be honest. I shaved my hands the other day and the rough touch of my skin against my…rod…left some red bruises.

When I opened the door, she was kneeling next to it, with her ear against it. She said she was listening to the grunts I made. What? She said it turned her on. Okay. I told her I didn't really like it, and that nothing happened. She looked a little angry when I did.

Next thing I knew, that door was slammed shut in my face. I tried to open it…but she had it locked from the outside somehow. Through the door…I was told to do it again. To do it to thoughts of her. So I did. And it worked. It felt good when it happened…but afterwards I didn't know how to feel. Everyday she would ask me to do it. I obliged.

She's my girlfriend, and I love her.

-Reez'

Flip. Flip. Flip.

ENTRY 15

'I don't even know how long I've been with this woman.

It has felt like forever. For good and bad reasons, honestly. Everyday, it's just…touch, touch, touch. Always me, never her. I feel trapped because she's all I have and all she has. She said she'd kill herself if I left. How am I supposed to feel about that?

She almost found this journal. I swear, if she did…the police would find two dead in her house. One, stabbed most likely. The other, suicide. I need to stop wearing my jacket around her. That, or leave the book at my place.

Today was the day she decided to look at it. My…you know…thing. Said it was an alright size. Really? Could have lied to me about it and I wouldn't have even known. She looked and sounded disappointed. Well, SORRY! I don't even want to be alive anymore.

I want to kill myself. But I can't. I have a reputation to uphold, and doing so would tarnish it. All these thoughts I now have…they're all sexual. I like it at the moment but afterwards…fuck. Can I not just tear my head off? Rip my brain out? It's all her fault. She has turned me into some erotic powerhouse for her own benefit.

All the touching…it's only around her. SHE wants to touch me. SHE wants to watch me touch myself. SHE wants to feel good. It's never about what I want. HER, HER, HER!!! It's like I'm a fucking sexdoll for her torturous pleasures! I know she's my girlfriend…but I don't know how long I want to be with her for. I'm just trapped.

I don't know if I love her.

Until next time. If there is a next time.

-Reez'

Flip. Flip. Flip. Flip. Flip.

ENTRY 20

'I feel nothing. I don't want to live. I've been used for everything; strung out like a wet rag.

Can death come sooner for me? I've done everything I can do. I did everything I've WANTED to do. Even before this girl, I felt like there was nothing left for me. Why must I stay living in this state of…HELL. For lack of a better Goddamn word. I don't even believe in a God. Not anymore, I don't.

I want to cut myself but thats too much for me. I want to just…die. Keel over and die type of death. Something natural, honestly. Maybe then this woman will think about what she's done to me. Maybe. I'm going to see her again tomorrow. I don't even want to. Not anymore. I can't even do what I want to do. It's either I get touched or she wants me to leave.

Maybe I should leave. I need to get out of this relationship. Do I even love her anymore? I don't think so. I just don't have the guts to.

Until the next time that I'm still alive.

Flip. The last entry he ever fully wrote about this girl.

ENTRY 21

'Today was it. The last I could take.

I tried to talk to her about it. A serious, mature conversation. She couldn't even handle that. I tried telling her all sorts of things. 'I never get to have my say.' 'You're just using me.' 'This is a one-sided relationship.' You know what I got in return? She would try to flash her breasts...or even her vagina. She thought it would work.

She even touched me trying to change my mind...but this time I reacted. I stopped her from doing anything more. She tried to get me to cry by recounting everything we did together. But in my head...all I had was hatred and regret. I just left. Is she still alive? I...don't know. I'm going to a beach tonight. Maybe I can just drown in the water surrounded by the loud banging and colorful sparks of the fireworks they're going to set off.

I'm alone...and I think this is it. I might be able to finally die. To be carried off into whatever waits for me beyond this life. If she's dead, good. She won't be able to do this to anyone else.

I don't love her. I love myself.

Until next time. Maybe.

-Reez'

I close the book, deciding not to reread it anymore. Every time I read that line about the beach...I want to tear up. I don't know precisely what day he was referring to, but...I bet it was the same beach where I met him. Just not the same day. The moment I met him, he was sitting alone on the coarse sand...watching the waves slowly settle down. I saw him beyond the crowd I was standing in. He gently stood up and took one step near the ocean. He was only...a few feet away, I believe?

I just remember running over to him...he was cute. His face was, at least. I didn't care about his body. Only his face. The colors and shades from the fireworks bounced off his face...and I fell in love. To think that he could have been seconds away from...I don't even want to think about it. And I never did things to him like that...vile woman did. I helped him. I made him happy. The following few entries are about days with me...and he was never sad, angry, or uncomfortable.

He truly loved me.

And I truly loved him.

Why did I lose him so soon? I hate reading this. I just miss him more every time I do. I saved him from death once...but I couldn't do it twice. I was even with him when he died. Why? Why did this have to happen? I miss him. I miss Reez.

I miss MY Reez.

Now I wear his jacket…the same one he wore when it happened to him. All the things I keep rereading. But he never said the other girl ever wore it. Good. She doesn't deserve it. She didn't deserve him. I hope she's dead.

"JANX!" Imbue yells from the captain's quarters. I hate calling it that, but he insists I do. I'd instead it be called the cabin or something much more straightforward. Whatever I honestly hope to be gone from him soon. I don't hate him; he's just getting a little much for me. Too energetic. Maybe I'm just too weary all the time now. I'm still traveling this stupid path that the weird purple lady told me to go on.

I've already hit the burning planet…Loca turned into that one. The dripping black sludge was probably Stalis? I'm hoping the endless sea of water is Secula since I can just leave Imbue's company once we land and figure out what I'm doing. As for the brain in a space of black…that must be my end goal. The Eternal Brain, as Meiv called it.

—

Walking down the ship's ramp into the dark, rainy city of Vasser, I brace myself for the complete downpour in front of me. The smell of rain is obviously vital. A heavy fog envelopes the buildings beyond the concrete bridge I now find myself walking on, but it does not extend to the vast ocean behind me. In all actuality, the combination of fog and constant rain causes the city to be

93

highly dark most of the time, even if it's day out. I did my research on the way here.

Green torches dot the flat gray bridge, a way to keep yourself from falling off the wall-less platform. I begin to pass through the highly dense outer layer of fog, where I can barely see the dim light of the torches. I try my best to keep moving forward. It's a short bridge but a long trip since I stroll to avoid hitting anyone or falling off.

Finally, I reach the city's outskirts, where bright neon lights shine through the gray clouds. Rain clashes against the metal buildings, where tall skyscrapers tower over the thin alleyways where the poor live. The showcase of the rich versus the poor is clearly evident here. Shops of various imported goods shine with murky green lights, which contrast the black and brown colors of the infrastructure.

It's all dreary, looking around at what I can only describe as the slummy armpit of a rich world. Everyone started on the ground, and now only the elite see the sun. Now that I'm on this planet… let's hope it's the right one. I'm unsure what I'm looking for or where Imbue is, but I'm on my own from here on out. I think I should change first…try to fit in a little more.

~The Reunion~

"DISCOUNTED MAID ROBOTS! FIRST COME, FIRST SERVE!"

"We got all sorts of food! Come take a look!"

"TERMINAL ILLNESS MEDICINE HERE!"

Everywhere I walk, it seems like someone's yelling or trying to sell products. It honestly ranges from the most minor things to cures for some serious diseases. It's a superb trading community; it's a shame it has to be overshadowed literally and figuratively.

The streets are a dull gray that only pops due to the amount of color used in the lights for the bottom-level markets and advertisements. Rain pours down onto the streets as the smell of sewage bristles by every now and again. I wonder how inflated the economy down here is.

Walking around, I notice that I attract many heads on my travels. Now, I'm used to that, especially in my early days of being an assassin, but these heads are different. Their expressions are exciting and as if scanning my features to see if they've seen me before.

I pass it off as an old wanted poster, but one creature catches me off guard. A hyper, three-foot-tall Orugnic swings down from some broken metal scaffolding on my right. He lands in front of me, onto the ruined pavement path stretching miles between towering buildings, walls that progressively get cleaner the higher you look.

He reminds me precisely of Marz, which is jolting at first. He walks on his hind legs and the knuckles of his arms. His nougat-brown fur slowly dances on his back as a soft wind tangos with each strand. Two bulbous sea-blue eyes bulge out from his smooth, pale face. His tail drags along the ground as he approaches me with an unknown intention.

"Are you Janx?" he asks in a soft and high-pitched voice. He tilts his head as he asks.

"Yes," I respond, kneeling on the ground to be more on his level. "How do you know me?"

"I work for the medical center," he says, pointing to the scrap pile he just jumped from. At the top of the point, a shattered glass door is embedded into a purple-walled building stretching far into the clouds and beyond the surrounding infrastructure. No windows can be seen down here, but I can make out a few near where the building disappears into the clouds.

Light from beyond the door beckons me in, a mix of soft yellow and some hues of green, almost like a field of grass shining with the light from a bright, healthy sun. I look back at the Orugnic, who grabs onto one of my hands and pulls me toward the scrap pile. We both try our best to climb it, with the Orugnic being much better than I am, but I can reach the doors without any significant problems.

Walking into the medical center lobby, two light fixtures on either side are the source of the yellow and green. The yellow light, which is a chandelier, hangs down from the dirty black and white marble ceiling. A green, shattered lamp lies on the red carpet that lines the floor. A torn lampshade sits dormant a few feet away, slightly hiding behind a ripped black leather couch.

The stench of aged leather and ancient alcohol reeks around the room, and the barren purple walls drip with an unknown indigo fluid from the top corners. A perfectly square lobby, with only the aforementioned light fixtures and couch, along with a singular help desk a yard away. On either side, two silver elevator doors remain shut, with one being held together with about a hundred yellow 'OUT OF ORDER' posters.

The floor creaks as I walk, despite the carpet covering the hardwood material underneath. The Orugnic quickly speeds past me, flipping over the counter and holding up a clipboard from the other side. He places it on top of the dark brown countertop, where it clunks against the solidified wood. I take a look at the yellowed, ripped paper where I see my face, albeit from a few Loca sun rotations ago, and the words 'HAVE YOU SEEN ME?' at the top in bold red letters.

"Are you the authorities?" I quickly ask, stepping back in case I need to run. Who is this guy? How does he know me? Who's looking for me? The Orugnic slides the clipboard off, placing it below the countertop. He laughs and shakes his head as he does so, rubbing the top of his furry head back.

"No, Janx, I'm not here to take you in or

something," he says. "You came just in time. We were about to dispatch one of our visitors, who is looking for you. His name is Row-N."

"What?" I ask. I haven't seen him in so long. He survived Loca? "Where is he?"

"He's on one of the top floors, room number 1-22-A, Section 4-Right. Meiv's room," the Orugnic says. He hands me a folded piece of white paper from seemingly nowhere, and I unfold it to see a crudely drawn floor plan made with black ink and dotted with random light red smudges. He points to the top right of the map, where I see the numbers 1-22-A. "Right there."

"And you're telling me Row-N is there? He hasn't left yet?" I ask. I can't believe I will see him after this long…I hope he's been alright.

"Nope. The only entrance and exit is this one right here."

"Ok," I say, finishing the conversation. I walk to the right elevator, the one working, and it opens up to a cramped circular chamber with peeling wallpaper covered in a dirty cream color and faded flower illustrations. Stepping inside, the platform rocks, and I grab onto the exposed golden metal walls for support. The doors close before I can press any buttons, and it launches up the shaft. I stumble and crash onto the floor, where I feel the elevator's speed continue to rise as a beeping sound plays, most likely as I pass each floor.

I wait a few moments on the grimy floor of the

elevator as it finally begins to slow, to the point it completely stops and doesn't rock back and forth. I pull myself up with a broken railing on the far wall, and I cover my eyes as the doors open, and a bright yellow light shines through. I step out onto the calming solid ground of whatever floor I'm on, where windows line the hallway before me. I'm above the cloud line, and the golden sun brightly shines through, illuminating the dry corridor.

Time to find Row-N.

I walk through the hallway, passing the chirping noises coming from beyond the walls. It's calming up here, but it also feels lonely. There are no random people walking about or any ambient noise floating around beyond where I can see. It just feels…empty. Like a dream where I'm the only person left in the universe. It feels distressing.

Turning a corner, I come face to face with a stretched hallway that seems to continue far beyond my sight. I rub my hand against the dust-covered moldy walls, leisurely walking along as I read each room number. Large black blocks of text line the door frames, telling people passing by the room number, the section of the medical center it's in, and what doctor owns the space. About three doors down from the corner, I find Meiv's.

Room number 1-22-A, Section 4-Right, Doctor Phremon. Next to the door, a manila folder is held to the peeling wallpaper with a rusty spring. I look at the paper, and the words' MEIV: CRITICAL CONDITION' are written on the top in bold, red letters. I slowly take the folder off the wall, and the spring slowly cracks, and little brown flakes fall to the ground.

It has a soft touch to it. I rub my fingers across the front and brush off some dust particles and dirt. I slide some fingers between the file, pushing apart the sides to see the many photos and documents inside. Printed pictures of Meiv's face, cracked and shrouded in purple rocks. What happened to her?

"Is someone there?" I hear from the door on my right. I turn my head in a second due to the suddenness of the voice. Do I go over? Why not? Meiv can wait. I take a few steps on the creaky tile floor that honestly reeks of something dead. Room number 1-23-A, Section 4-Right, Doctor Phremon.

Before I'm able to see past the half-open door, I hold up the manila folder of the mystery person. In the same red lettering as before, I read 'ZEVERIAN: LIFE SUPPORT PHASE FIVE.' I've read that name somewhere…but where? I think for a moment, but I am unable to remember where I've heard Zeverian before.

A lightbulb flashes in my head as if a ghost whispered into my ear. I quickly throw the file back onto the wall, where the spring doesn't bounce back. It creeps back into the wall, where it dents the wooden infrastructure. I shove my hands into the inside pockets of Reez's jacket, where I pull out his journal. Flipping through the pages onto Entry 24, I read the name at the top.

Zeverian.

It's the girl that Reez wrote about. The one that….

As I put the book back into its pocket, I storm through the door. I push it open, and it bangs into the wall, and I can hear the spring-fall onto the ground behind me. As my eyes adjust to the bright sunlight bleeding through the windows on the far side of the room, I slowly get a look at the space around me.

Firstly, the smell of cleaning products and old people climb up my nostrils and the occasional beeping sounds of a heart rate monitor. The room's polished pastel green and blue colors are a shocking contrast to the dreary colors of the outside hallways. They give me a sense of calm and safety as I jog to a halt in the middle of the room. My angered demeanor is quickly abolished as I look upon Zeverian.

The room is empty. No beds line the walls, no pictures, no nothing. Just a heart rate monitor and an IV hooked up to a shriveled woman in a black steel wheelchair. Is this the same woman? I slowly finish the walk over to the girl, where I step on a singular chrome silver leaf. The crunch echoes through the room, and I see the woman's ears perk up.

"Is that you…Reez?" she asks in a soft, broken voice. Why is she asking for him? I walk around her to stand in front of the window she's looking out of. The sunlight shines off of her face…and I get a good look at her features. Cloudy green eyes...probably blind. Graying black hair, wrinkled skin, and a pale yellow body. She's covered in a weighted blue blanket, which protects everything under her neck.

"Reez is dead," I struggle to say. I hate saying it because I still don't want to accept it. The woman lets out a soft 'Oh,' and her eyelids droop down. "Did you know him?"

"Yes...a long time ago. I don't seem to remember exactly when...I lost track of time when I lost my sight." That confirms she's blind, then. "My time is near, and I sent out messages to people I knew. He was the only one that didn't show."

"I'm sorry," I hesitantly say. Am I sorry? This is the girl I read about so much...right in front of me. Dying. How should I feel? Do I forgive her? She didn't hurt me...but she broke Reez. Does she even know what she did?

"I hope he can forgive me," Zerverian slowly spurts out. "I know I hurt him. He never explicitly said it...but I could tell. I was just so young...and so was he. Our brains weren't developed and I took advantage of it. And of him."

She does know. And she's sorry.

"And if he is dead...I hope he was able to find it in himself to mentally forgive me before his death. I know I struggled to forgive myself. But I do now," she continues to say. "Don't hold grudges, my dear. You sound

102

young…like how I was when I was with him. We all die someday. We should all die with no worries…so that when we're carried away by Death, we accept him as he does us."

"You're very philosophical," I say. I wasn't expecting a lesson today.

"It happens with age," she responds. The tapping of rain against the window begins to echo through the room as the sun rises higher. "Thank you. He was the only person I didn't know how they felt anymore. Even though I still am not sure if we are on the same page about each other…I did care about him. And I know he did too. I hope he still did even in his death. All my worries are gone. My head is empty…and I don't mind."

The beeping of the monitor slowly increases in length as I look out of the window into the crashing blue waves. The pink sand below is dotted with little black specs; obviously, people going about their day. I guess the hospital was built near a beach so the dying could watch the only nature left at this point.

Isn't that odd? They don't even know that someone is dying right next to them. They are just enjoying their life. I'm reminded of Magona and how he has suspiciously not shown up in a while. Maybe he's dead? Either that or these people won't be able to continue their bloodlines. I hope not.

The beeping turns into a long melodic noise, and I look down at the ground. I hear some rustling behind me, but I do not look back. I gaze at the pristine environment until I remember that I need to return to Meiv's room. I quickly turn around, seeing an empty wheelchair with a fallen blanket. Can I hate her anymore?

"I forgive you," I say. She hurt him…but I know that Reez would forgive her. I should too. The monitor shuts off as I walk past it, and the windows close, shutting off the outside light. I step through the clean room, the silver leaf sticking to the bottom of my feet. Crunch, crunch, crunch.

"Room's open," I hear from the hallway outside as I walk through the door. I close it behind me, and the soft click of the lock flows through my ears. A few doctors of various species rush past me, donning spotless white robes. They look at me as they hurry on their way, quietly laughing as one stretches around me to grab the fallen spring and manila folder.

Do they care for the people that they supposedly 'care' for? I doubt it. I should get back to Meiv's…Row-N is waiting for me. I walk back to the next door over, where I slowly creak it open to see Row-N's hulking form sitting low beside the desolate bed that Meiv rests on. The rest of the room is bare. What's the point of these rooms, then?

"Please, no visitors," Row-N says, noticing me walk in. I take a long look at his weathered body, looking much worse than the last time I saw him. His dirty brown and gray metal face still has the usual two red eyes and the six small deep blue ones above them, but about half on either side are cracked and have lost their color. Both of his linen-colored horns are broken off, and only the trunk of them remains. His body is mostly scrap metal held together with various dull-colored ropes and cloth rags. One of his arms, along with his left foot, is completely missing.

He kneels next to Meiv's bedridden body, and her skin is flushed of all colors besides the purple crystals that infect her body. Her skin and clothes are all monotone, an empty shade of light gray. Row-N's body sparks and shutters as he jumps out, actually noticing it's me. He runs over and wraps his one arm around me, and I wrap mine around him. I can't help myself as I begin to silently break down.

"You made 8088-Y to save me?" I ask through rivers of tears. Row-N pats my head as he responds.

"Both Reez and I knew about your true power…and I knew that you could possibly help in this battle," he says. "And Reez is the one that requested I better my robotic research in order to provide a 'bodyguard' for you."

"I'm sorry, but I don't know where he is," I say. "I left them a long time ago."

"I know. He hasn't been responding to any of my distress calls," Row-N responds. He releases from our hold and points with his only hand to a row of beds on the right side of the entrance door. I walk over to the blood-stained yellow mattresses to see three beds, two full and one

105

empty. The empty one has a deep hole in the middle, with the edges burned away by some sort of fire or lava.

The first of the two bodies is a five-armed creature with skin paler than a dead man. His face is frozen in a state of shock, eyes, and mouth both wide open. His arms are all outstretched in different directions, with trickles of neon green blood down to the tip of each finger. Half of his body is covered with a dirtied white cloth, but his chest is exposed to show off the gaping hole in the middle.

The hole is about the size of a powerful blast of a firing weapon, possibly a Saitun Rifle. The second of the two bodies are adorned with a sadly ruined dress created from shining white crystals that look as though they were crafted from the heavens. Her skin is a soft mint color, but her neck ends in a jumble of skin tissue, blood, and bone fractures. Her head is completely gone.

"Who are these people?" I ask. "Did you know them?"

He grabs onto my shoulder and pulls me back, and I break my focus on the bodies to look at Row-N. "We were traveling here when a man boarded our ship just miles away from the atmosphere of this planet," Row-N explains. "He demanded to check our ship for someone, but we tried to tell him we only had cargo. He killed these two, incapacitated a third, and brutally injured Meiv here."

"Who is he? Do you know?" I ask. I look over at Meiv, whose crystals shine slightly brighter than before. I tilt my head as Row-N turns his. We both stare as the light definitely grows, and purple floods the previously yellow room. The sun outside fades away, and the blue sky cracks and bleeds with lavender shine. The ground around me rumbles, and Row-N seems to notice it too. We both fall to the ground as reality seems to crumble, with the purple cracks forming through everything and the building and sky disintegrating as we pass through the floor.

"WHAT IS HAPPENING??!" I yell out as my voice echoes through the smoky dark purple void we find ourselves falling in. I look around at the empty space, and besides Row-N and I, the only other thing is the floating body of Meiv. Her crystals strobe with lights that almost blind me. A wind current whisks around me, and it circles the glowing girl.

"Excuse me?" a masculine voice echoes from behind. I spin myself around as the wind grows more violent, and the noises of groans and crying loom around me. I see a man wearing a dark brown tunic and dress pants; shoes that could reflect any light; wet, combed-back black hair; strikingly blue eyes that could disappear into an ocean; and a sharp jawline. He holds out a hand to me, standing as if he's on an invisible platform.

I pull myself through the whirlwind of purple winds, throwing my arm forward, and as our fingers touch, my body straightens out. The winds and horrific noises cease, and the darkness lights up. I quickly look around, my hand still adjoined to this man, as I find myself in some sort of green paradise. A ticking clock tower looms beyond a forest of tall, dark brown trees whose branches bend down to form a triangular look to them. I hear chirping birds and a distant choir of angelic voices as if I had just entered the gates of the afterlife.

I look up and down at the man a few times, scanning his body language to try and understand who this guy is. Am I dead? What the hell just happened? Where's Row-N and Meiv? Who is this man, and how did he appear in that purple void?

"Trying to understand if I mean harm or not?" he asks. I stand dumbfounded.

"Y-yes," I stutter out. He knew? A friendly smile creeps up on his angled face, and he chuckles.

"I wouldn't be surprised; you're also probably wondering how I was able to pull you out of that...," the man makes weird spinny motions with his hands as he talks. "Purple glob."

Also my exact thoughts.

"It's an air pocket that travels through small air molecules in order to traverse extensive stretches of space. It can launch itself so far that I believe you can go from one galaxy to another with just one jump," the man explains. "Once the connection to a molecule is broken, the pocket will blast through any amount of space forever until the nearest molecule is found."

"Who are you?" I yell out before he can continue. He looks right into my eyes as I stand slightly crouched, seeing the fluffy white clouds swirl around the glowing blue sky. Connected to the base of the ticking clock, rickety brown wooden bridges crisscross with each other. I see the purple orb blipping in and out of visibility on top of the bridges, growing closer and closer to the other side of the clock tower: a sprawling base of light gray stone with domes of shining glass atop the square shape.

"I am Mic Braidee, and welcome to the valley," he says. He turns to the bridge, where my eyes are glued to. "I never thought I'd see her again."

"You know her?" I ask. "We should probably catch up, my friend is still stuck in that bubble."

"Yeah, we go back a little. I'd rather not discuss it. If we are able to catch up to her, I just need any part of me to touch the outer edge," Mic says. "Once an outside force comes into contact with the energy surrounding the orb, it'll stop in place."

From the glass domes atop the stone base, a flash of purple light shines out and paints the sky a dark lavender. An invisible blast of force pushes through the grassy plains and hills, pushing Mic and me onto the ground. I fall onto the pillowy floor, blades of grass poking the back of my head.

"You," Mic says, pointing at me from the ground. I turn my head to see him holding onto his forehead, shiny red blood dripping between his fingers. "Go. I'll catch up."

"Do you need assistance?" I ask. I reach to my stomach to grab a medical patch, but as I feel the heavy jacket, I remember I'm not wearing my corset anymore.

He shakes his head and some droplets of blood splash around. I can see the veins in his fingers and arm bulge as he tightens the grip on his head. He points at the base momentarily as he lowers his body onto the ground.

I turn to the stone building as deep black smoke begins to bellow out of a gargantuan hole in the front of the base. It continues to grow as more and more stone bricks fall, smashing against each other and landing in the flowing blue river surrounding the base. Shit. What the fuck did that girl do? Meiv…the crystal woman. She better not have hurt Row-N.

I scan the area for any entrance since I can see where all the bridges begin and end. There are no doors, no windows I can easily access, and no gates. The only open area I can see is a few yards to my right, near the base of the clock tower. A white, fenced-off garden with a towering fountain in the middle of the greenery. An orange portal sits at the closest end, while a slanted bridge stretches opposite it into the clock tower's dark gray stone base.

That'll be my destination.

~The Valley~

Death kneels down before a moribund Felishe, one that bleeds from the left eye. He looks up into the dark ceiling, his body thrashing as he loses his life. Death pulls down his brown hood, looking upon the Felishe. Dark gray fur…scars all over…and the gleam of life in his eye still there.

"Death…is that…you?" the Felishe asks out. His remaining eye doesn't move at all; it stays on the concrete above. Death doesn't answer. "Don't…take her…please."

"Who?" Death finally says. He looks away from the fleeting Felishe; toward a bullet-ridden Canilupus bleeding out under the window.

"Janx…just please let her live…."

"If she follows the trail, she can wish you back. She can change anything," Death says.

"Don't let her…bring me back."

"You'll be able to tell her yourself."

~~

Death is something I've come to know. Not as a person but as a concept. I used to be desensitized to killing and people dying. But now…I feel like I have more humanity to me. I don't know what it is. But seeing Meiv's skin burned to her bones did something to me.

Patches of pale purple skin stretching across her blackened bones…the eggplant-colored crystals in her body now gone, leaving ragged holes of whitened lavender

111

muscle and exposed veins. Eyes rolled to the back of her head, with now two black orbs staring up at the charred library ceiling. The top of her head is marked with bulging scars, and the lower half of her face is completely burned to the skeletal jaw. From her elbows to the tips of each finger is nothing but bone.

Her body lays in a newly created ditch in the middle of the nougat wood floor. Around us, rows of books on shelves that reach almost fifteen feet high. Pages float to the ground, the shredded edges brown and yellowed. The fire has already ceased; the last of it danced away as I walked under the chiseled wooden archway at the top of crumbled stone stairs.

Outside the enclosed five-foot library, a walled-in field of gray awaits, lit by singular torches dotted around the walls. Inside the base rows of stone staircases, hidden wall entrances to other locations, clear windows that display a Northern blue ocean along a sandy coast, among other design oddities. Embedded into the corner of one of the four tower cobble walls of the base is a small double gate, which leads out to the maze of bridges.

The glow of the golden lights shines upon the empty rooms, making everything seem more lonely. Nobody roams any of the stretching halls or rickety bridges. The only life I've stumbled across has been Mic. I haven't seen him since I ran in. I believe he may still be out there.

Luckily, Row-N is still alive. I wouldn't say he was utterly safe since he didn't come out unscathed. He lies against the library's archway; the lights in his eyes are dimmer than before. His lone arm rests upon his bulky chest as I look upon its dents and dirtied silver color. On the left side of his neck, a small panel is broken off, revealing a void of black with a single bright red tube running through. He's still alive; I can literally feel it.

It pulses as orange lights pass in between the tube's fleshy walls. I rest two of my fingers against it, feeling the vein-like object flow upwards toward the head of Row-N. I grab onto his head, feeling for an opening, when one of the glass eyes shatters. Is this some sort of backup mechanism to stay alive?

I throw my arms up, glass blasting past them. Cuts drag along my skin, and the blood splatters onto my face. A few shards are embedded in my arms and shoulders, but I lower them to see light gray smoke emitting from the eye. I don't even know if there are any medical personnel on this planet...where is that Mic guy?

"Row, are you alright?" I quietly ask. I brush my hand through the air, wafting the smoke away. The shape and slight detail of Row-N's metallic face poke through the gray as I examine the shards lodged in my arms. Pieces of clear glass, now stained red with the leaking blood. They range in size from a few small ones to a dozen sizable chunks. No time to pull them out right now.

113

A small, bite-sized hand grasps the rim of Row-N's eye, pulling up from beyond the dark interior of the head. Two glowing piss-yellow eyes break through the smoke as a teeny-tiny creature struggles to free itself. I quickly grab onto Row-N's metallic skull, pushing my thumbs into both eye holes. My right thumb efficiently clears through the missing glass, but my left crack through the right eye.

I brace the pain and push my right thumb harder against the cracking glass, the shards cutting deep into my skin and sending burning feelings through my hand. A section of my brain pulses, clearly telling me that I need to stop, but I press on. When I feel the cold steel of Row-N's head, I pull it apart. Or at least, I try.

I strain my arms, trying to pull the metal apart. I take my arms back momentarily, letting my jacket slide off onto the ground. Placing my hands back, I see my veins pop from my skinny pale arms as the creature's upper body plops forward, its hand grabbing onto my right thumb. Its four chubby brick-red fingers latch and wrap fully around my thumb. I slowly retract my hand back; the creature continues to hold on. I watch as a scrimpy little THING is pulled out from the smoking Row-N head.

Is this Row-N himself? The mind that controls the machine? His face has a triangular shape to it, with the nose and mouth conjoined at the tip. Both eyes lie on top of the mound, fleshy eyelids stretching back to reveal the hot pink ring that circles cloudy white pupils. His thin, pencil-shaped body contorts as he climbs onto my right shoulder, hugging my neck as the smoke clears. His mechanical husk lies dormant as we both let out a harsh sigh.

"She almost activated my self-destruct," Row-N's tiny body says. His voice is high and quiet, but I can easily hear him since he's beside my ear. "If my suit receives enough damage, it'll send out a copper-borax mixed solution into the air that will immediately heat up and explode."

"How close were you that time?" I ask.

"Too close. I think I stunted the destruct but I'm not climbing back in to check," Row-N responds. "I need a new suit."

"Are you two alright?" Mic asks, lumbering in from the open archway entrance. Bright beams of gleaming yellow light shine through as the sun outside sets. They cut through the gray stone columns that hold up the fortress walls, casting them in heavy shadow.

"Yes, just some scratches here and there," I respond jokingly.

"I wish I could have presented a better introduction to my land, but alas here we are," Mic says. "Janx, correct?"

"Yes."

"I heard a lot about you," Mic says with a friendly smile. He reaches a bony hand out. "Death whispers enough to talk one's ear off."

"Who are you and how did we end up here?"

115

—

I wait for Mic to return after dragging me to a hill across one of the significant wooden bridges dotting the land. A beautiful kiss of wind rubs against my cheeks, and I feel an odd sense of warmth. Five chiseled stone graves stick out before me from the green grass. Fragments of pink blades remain, but the warmth of spring brings forth the green. Four of the stones blur in my mind because one…one stands out. Labeled 'The Soldier.' Underneath the bold identifying text reads a sentence that I'm not sure how to fully feel about it. It reads:

'Do not bring me back; I know I will see her again.'

Me?
Is he talking about me?
A soft wind blows around me, wailing in my ears. I feel the presence of someone watching me, but looking around the area, I see no one. That is until I glance at the bridge. Two figures traverse the rickety structure, but I recognize one on the left side as Mic. Next to him, on his right, is a bulking beast of shining golden color.

They make their way up to me as I set my eyes on the almost eight-foot-tall Row-N. Golden armor with purple highlights at the joints, sharp edges, horns around the upper body, and chains of gold wrapped around his neck and waist. His body is much bulkier than before, and

116

the suit is probably stronger as well. The helmet is the same shape and design as his previous suit, albeit with gold plating and purple eyes.

"I like the new look," I say. He throws up a thumbs-up as he turns back and waddles down the bridges. "Is he off somewhere?"

"He's still in training. I equipped some new additions, like a built-in gatling gun on his right arm, a jetpack, and NO self-destruction device this time," Mic explains. "I've been around for a long time, I know how to handle machinery."

"Is your head alright?" I ask Mic as I see Row-N enter the stone base from the corner of my eye. His golden suit shines brightly in the setting sun. The sky grows purple and dark, and the stars are oddly visible already.

"Oh, yes. Don't worry about that," Mic replies, patting his hand on the large gashes around his scalp. "Just some unpleasant memories."

"Did you get in a fight?" I ask. "You don't seem like a fighter. I'd expect you to sign peace treaties and negotiate with others, honestly."

"Well, that is me," Mic says. He plops down onto the grass, almost bouncing as he does. "How long have you been around for, Janx?"

"Probably not as long as you," I reply. "Shouldn't your hair be gray by now?"

Mic lets out a chuckle and a smile.

"I am that old, aren't I? I've been around almost as long as life itself," Mic explains. "You'd think some would love the immortality aspect of it. But it gets lonely after a while."

"Why can't you die?" I ask, expecting a jokey answer-back. Mic instead turns to the setting sun, and his smile fades.

"I want to die," Mic says. He pulls up one of his sleeves to reveal scars and cuts all over his skin, some held together with metal shards and needles. "And I've tried. I've done everything. The fish at the bottommost part of these blue oceans practically know my name. I wear rope around my neck as a decor piece now. I am my own knife block."

"I'm sorry," I say, regretting asking him in the first place. He quickly throws a hand out.

"Oh, please. I hear that all the time. 'I'm sorry you can't die,' or 'I'm sorry you hurt yourself,' or...," he pauses. "Or that they're sorry for leaving you. Have you noticed how empty this place is?"

"Well, I thought maybe it's an off-map planet," I respond. He shakes his head. I can see his watery eyes shimmer in the light.

"Everyone I have known and loved has died. Lovers, friends...everyone. I've never had parents. I've outlived my greatest of grandchildren. Most people believe in the 'Realm of Death,' or whatever bullshit place you go after you die. But is it real? If it was, they'd all visit me. It's a curse to live like this."

"Do you know why you can't die?" I ask after a moment of silence. He shakes his head no.

"Everyone has a path in life," he responds, wiping his right eye. "Everyone has a set goal. What's left after that goal? Nothing. I thought I've done everything I could. At this point, I'm done. I haven't achieved anything since before Earth I shut down."

"You think death happens when someone has made all their set decisions? What if they die before or a long time after?" I ask.

"I think that people dying is the final decision they make. They don't even do it consciously. Whether it be from natural causes, or getting hit by a bullet," Mic explains. "If someone wanted to do something, but died before they could, it means they were never set to do it. And like I said, sometimes that final decision is dying. Fate…or time…or something…leads people to the right place and right time to die."

"What about people in relationships? Shouldn't being together forever be that decision keeping them alive?" I ask as I begin to freak out. Reez didn't die for nothing…fate didn't do that. He was shot. I saw it. I know why and how it happened.

"That's what happens," Mic says, pointing his finger to Reez's grave. I turn to it, staring at the chiseled stone that bears the name of the one I miss.

"Who buried him here?" I ask, kneeling down before the grave. My legs softly land, the sides enveloped in blades of sharply green grass. Mic looks up at the stars as the sun vanishes behind the distant hills topped with white snow.

"I did," Mic says. I quickly turn my head toward him.

"What?" I let out. "How did you get his body? Who gave it to you? HOW MUCH DID YOU PAY?"

"Please…calm down," Mic says in a defeated voice. "All these bodies were brought to me. For a reason. I had nothing to do with their deaths or anything. I have another two I'll need to bury one day. I'm not looking forward to it. I can show you the bodies; there's an underground room below us with windows into the graves."

"No, it's alright," I say, calming myself down with deep breaths. "Who gave them to you?"

"Death," Mic says. A ghostly gust of wind whisks around us, the name being carried away as distant sounds of crashing slice through to our ears.

"Do you hear that?" I ask. A metallic noise bursts out from the ravines surrounding the base's back. A sky blue light emits from the darkness as a bright pink object looms above in the distant void of space. "Was that there before?"

I stand up at the same time as Mic crouches over. We both speed-walk over the hills, circling the backyard ravines. The sound of a motor being started and the wind up of turbines blows out air, pushing Mic and me backward. We stand our ground, however, as something rises up.

"How?" Mic yells out. What is it? What are we looking at?

"What is that?" I yell over to Mic.

"That's a specially made Turbo-Socking Model 85 JetStreamer," he responds. "Complete with a full arsenal of weaponry. I made it during the Battle of Stoean. Specifically the latter half, when Mondio Sulez was defeated and the industrial tech weapons were permitted in battle. I had to defend my home somehow."

The ship turns toward us as the triple blue-flame thrusters point the opposite way. I squint my eyes as a spotlight atop the base shines down a gleaming red beam onto the shining jet. Its sleek, silver, triangular body glows bloody; the umbrella of light turns to shadow under the ship's curved underside. Two thin wings on both sides point about a yard out in either direction, holding a metal thruster on the edges. They're on some sort of hinge; they probably move up and down during travel. They both angle downward, holding the jet in the air.

The pointed front of the jet holds an angled cockpit window blocked by a shadowy fog on the inside. The red spotlight continues to shine down on the ominous fighter craft as I feel a drop on my left shoulder. I look down to see the blades of pink and green grass being shot with water droplets. Rain?

"It shouldn't be raining," Mic says from next to me, his eyes still trained on the jet. He stands in a defensive stance, with one leg back and both arms held up forward. "This planet doesn't have a proper water cycle. I had to import all these seas from other planets."

"Then how is it raining?" I ask. I feel another drop on my forehead as I turn my head up. I wipe the drop away with my hand and look down at my fingers to see what it is, noticing the dark color of the liquid as Mic fills me in.

"This is blood," he says as my head realizes the red color of the droplet. "I think it's our time to leave."

Buzz.

What was that?

I look at Mic, who pulls a small black box out of an inside pocket in his suit. It buzzes in his hand, and he taps the top a few times until a dim baby blue light shines upon his face.

"K-T?" he calls out. "Where are you?"

"NOT--SAFE! GET--NOW BEFO--CAN!" a static, broken-up voice glitches out from the box. "MAGONA IS--OMING!"

Before we can react, a sharp blast, complete with a blinding flash of white and orange, cut through my vision. Leaves splatter my face as my eardrums pop; a tree behind me falls. I wipe the charred leaves off my face, letting them glide to the wet ground as I look over my shoulder to

122

see a crater in the ground. One big enough to bury an army of five hundred men. Bright red-orange fire mixes and dances in the blood rain, the light shining off my wet, glossy body.

"He's getting away!" Mic yells out. I look back to see the ship quietly blasting upward with a stream of baby blue light following behind. "If he gets too close…."

"What?" I yell out. The looming orb of pink shines momentarily as I watch the jet fly. "What will happen?"

"There's a shield up there!" Mic yells. "If he gets too close… it'll destroy the-!"

BOOM.

CRACK.

CRASH.

SHATTER.

CRASH.

CRACKLE.

The spotlight shines up from the ground, broken off the base's roof by the falling jet. It all happened so fast. I wasn't even expecting it. Wait… I'm lying on the ground. When did I get here? Where is Mic? Crackling continues in my ears, and I watch the burning rubble of the jet shake as cracks form on the window from the inside. Something is trying to escape. The pilot?

POUND.

CRACK.

Something is trying to escape.

POUND.

CRACK.

Or is it someone?

POUND.

CRACK.

That one sounded heavy.

POUND.

SHATTER.

The red light shining up from the fallen spotlight illuminates the gray smoke as a shadowy figure emerges. A body, albeit slightly out of shape. Two legs. Two arms. A face; one that does not look like a human. Two bent ears at the top…one lower than the other. Rough patches of hair dot the surrounding skin of the head. Something that looks like drool drips down from the darkened face.

"Who are you?" I yell out. Behind the smoking pile of fire and metal, tall trees of brown wood and green leaves shake in the heavy wind. I watch as the white stars in the sky disappear. One by one. The pink ball grows closer.

"Janx…you should've let me kill you…you would've saved yourself the trouble…," the figure calls out. He jumps from the rubble and onto the ground, where he waddles toward me with his left leg bent inward and one arm at a ninety-degree angle backward. The voice…I know him.

"You?" I call out. He steps into the light. His face is illuminated. Patches of darkened gray fur. Two crimson eyes…one covered in scratches. A baby blue nose on the tip of a crooked snout. Stitches, staples, and all sorts of pins stick through his fur, holding his face together. The blood spots and red markings around the cuts and gashes spill blood against the ground, disproving my earlier drool comment.

"Ace?" I say. I can see through some of the large openings in his skin, and the inside of his head has been stuffed with some sort of cardboard and plastic mashup. Where is his skull? "What happened to you? How are you still alive?"

"Please, Janx. I don't even want this to go on anymore. It's all over. Everyone will die; even you," Ace calls out in a distressed voice. "Take your life now, please. I woke up here...and I can't die. I can't. I CAN'T!"

He throws his arms up and falls to his knees as the blood rain splatters against him. He lands by my feet, and I feel Mic's heavy arms grab onto my shoulders and pull me away. I'm dragged through the wet grass, my ass feeling the coldest it's ever felt.

"We need to go," I hear Mic say. It sounds slow. Everything feels slow. What is Ace talking about?

"Please, Janx!" he yells, reaching an arm out toward me. Mic continues dragging me, not even looking back. He could've killed me. Why didn't he?

"Inside will be safe. We must defend ourselves," Mic says. His voice drowns out Ace's as he brings me across one of the lower-level bridges into a cobblestone hallway decorated with red torches. Who is coming?

125

—

A hall of ships. Is that what we are to defend ourselves with?

At the bottom of the ravine where Ace flew out, a row of different models of ships line the cavernous walls. Jagged stone and uneven dirt reach all the way to the sky, or at least that is how it looks. The lack of natural light anymore definitely does not help my depth perception.

"What are we going to do?" I ask Mic as I rub my left elbow. I seem to have gotten a bruise on it at some point. Not sure how.

"Escape. A few of these ships can pass through stationary vortex energy fields," Mic explains. "It's what the shield is made of and it's all natural. It just has to do with-"

"I really don't care. Can you just give me the rundown?" I cut him off. "You're gonna throw us two on a ship with you and then what? Where to?"

I point to Row-N, whose gold armor shines in the…actually…how is it shining right now? There is barely any light, and the only sources that could be the reason are too dim to produce the amount of blinding shine that I am seeing right now.

"We just were attacked by an enemy, and you wanna stop for a chitchat?" Row-N asks. He doesn't sound angry at me…but not happy either. I count about seven triangular-shaped ships, one rectangular one, and three orb-like vehicles. If he could sell these, he'd be the

126

wealthiest man in the universe. We walk across the uneven stone floor, and I look back to the door we came out of. A wooden door with metal framing stuck in the middle of a cobblestone wall. On the other side is a beautiful room with a lovely wooden floor and plenty of medical beds. On this side, the wall is quickly covered in the dirt that lines the ravine walls.

"Here we go," Mic says. "We'll be heading to a friend of mine's."

He holds his arm out to one of the orb...things. It's perfectly spherical and is coated with a glossy black paint job. He wipes his hand against the side, and smoke is released with a puff from a door frame shape that emits from the orb. A rectangle of black slowly moves down onto the ground, revealing a bright light from inside.

"The Aioncle-36moelB. At least it's a working title," Mic says. "The design of the outside is to withstand SVE fields."

"Does it fly fast?" I ask. Mic nods his head up and down. With a smile, of course.

"Let's go in."

I climb the perfectly sized steps into the orb, and Mic follows behind. A soft cushion wraps around the curved white walls inside the claustrophobic area. I sit down, and the couch folds and contorts to match the shape of my ass and the bottom of my thighs. Mic sits opposite me, giving enough space for Row-N to sit between us. Where is he?

127

I look outside the ship, where Row-N stands at the base of the steps. He faces toward the base, his back to us. What is he doing?

"What are you doing?" I yell out.

"Something feels off," Row-N says. He turns his head toward us but looks off to the side. "Ace coming back has to mean something more."

"So? Get on the ship," Mic commands. Row-N shakes his head. He slowly raises his arms up to his chest, where he cracks off his golden chest plate, letting it fall to the ground. It slams against the stone, and he reveals his original suit of silver.

"We agreed not to wear that again!" Mic yells out. "The self-destruct mechanism is still set to blow with any hit!"

"Then I'll dodge every attack. Someone is waiting in that building. Ace cannot be the only one here," Row-N says. He grabs onto the bottom of his golden mask and struggles to push it off. He cracks the mask, bends some of the metal, and throws it completely off. It clangs to the ground a few feet away. All that's left above the neck is a small pillar with Row-N's actual body sitting on the top.

"ROW-N, YOU GET IN THIS SHIP NOW!" I yell out. He is NOT going to go back. No offense to Mic, but I am not going to stay with this man. "PLEASE!"

"Janx. Calm yourself. I am Row-N, creator of my Leathean Machines. I also excel in medicine. I can fix myself up anytime," Row-N laughs. He throws his left arm

128

to his side, where a panel opens up, and a golden Gatling gun spins out. He holds it up as he looks up at the looming stone base. "Goodbye, Jan X."

I don't bother correcting him. I know he did it on purpose. I try to step up to jump out, wanting to join him. But Mic holds an arm out, slamming me right in the stomach. I fall backward, holding my stomach as the door closes.

"ROW-N!" I yell out. He doesn't even look back. The door seals closed as we suddenly blast upward. The walls of the orb blink into an LED screen of everything around us. I look down at the orb's floor to see the base shrink as we fly away from it.

"Will he be safe? Is there really someone in there?" I ask.

"We'll come back for him," Mic says, leaning his head against the wall and closing his eyes. "This place is the most secur-"

Boom.

It wasn't even loud.

But the blast spun our ship around the planet. The screen's view turned from the land to the colors mixing. Mixing into lines that turned into a singular color. I felt the speed; it pulled me in every direction at once with the weight of a million tons. We were spinning in every direction, heading every way, going at every speed. Right before the blast hit us, I saw the base. On the top was a

129

glass dome, and I watched inside as a cloud of green flames blasted through the top. That was Row-N.

He let himself get hit.

I don't feel the same as when Reez was killed.

But it is close. After I was lost and found someone, I knew again. After all, he fathered me in a way.

I should've killed myself when I had the chance. I know I've had multiple.

Ace was right.

Everyone will die.

~The Revelation~

"The Hunter is in the deep reaches of the monster mine," Magona responds. He turns and looks out the ruined clock tower wall, into the distance past the dark brown observation tower and blazing stone base, all the way to a bundle of leafless black trees. They cover a small island near the vast dark blue ocean. The only connection to the mainland is from a small shiny red wooden bridge extending from the base of the observation tower.

"Why down there?" Airn asks. She walks past Magona and rests her hands on a raised, jagged piece of silver steel that wobbles with each soft kiss of the wind.

"He must be contained until we do the blood transfusion," Magona answers. "Hence, why I moved Al-X's body."

"Right," Airn says. She looks up into the sky where The Eternal Brain shines brightly with the cracks that have formed. She thinks to herself about what will happen when Magona enters the Brain…but even the act of thinking about it hurts. For a moment, she just wishes she could be free, but at this point, where would she retreat to? All that's left is The Valley and The Eternal Brain.

A shrieking alarm sounds through the emptiness as a subtle breeze whisks around them. Magona feels the change in the atmosphere through his sword. The blade is now intertwined with his arteries and veins and has grown a new tube that connects right into his head. He's gone

131

insane ever since he finished the blade. He's been controlled by the sword. Told what to do. Where to go.

The sword is in control now. Not Magona. Even Airn knows this; she's seen the transformation. How Magona's skin has gotten paler, his eyes more white. As if he's been dead for some time and is now a walking corpse, being kept alive by a sentient weapon of orange glow. As Magona's breath deepens from the ever-increasing cold environment, Airn looks out into the sky.

The brain is close. The cracks continue to form as the white light remains the only source of light around. The rest of the universe is gone…and only the space around The Valley and The Eternal Brain remains. She sees a new light form in the middle of the sky. A beam of white shines down into the middle of a murky black trench, where a swirling mix of blue and black appears at the top of the light.

"Is that The Seventh?" Airn asks, watching as a blurry block of charred material blasts from the wormhole. The falling object slams into the ground, immediately stopping as soon as it hits the hard dirt. It spins as it nosedives into the black soil. The lime inferno atop the stone base roars with growth as sounds of infrastructure collapsing echo throughout The Valley.

"No," Magona says. He stands at the other end of the clock tower, watching the base burn. His pale, almost transparent face reflects the neon green as the skin around his lipless, gaping mouth dries from lack of saliva. Is he even still alive? There's no way he can be... he's so pale, yet there's not even a single vein on his head.

"Should we start the blood transfusion?" Airn asks.

"Yes," Magona says, his voice raspy. They both take the spiral staircase in the middle of the clock tower; down to the charred ground, where they both begin their journey to the lab. Airn walks across the ruined floor, avoiding the fallen cogs and shattered gears.

~~

Despite being destroyed beyond recognition, the clock tower ticks, yet it still stands. The black land and dark, leafless trees sway in the soft but uncomfortable wind. The sky is empty of any color, lacking stars and bordering plants. The only thing in view is the pink, brain-like landmass that displays a large crack in the middle, which bleeds white light.

The orb burns orange behind us as I carry Mic's arm over my shoulder. We stumble through the muddy ground, past dancing flames of green. The cobblestone base, just barely out of view, roars in a lime inferno. The outer green layer mixes with the internal white flames, causing a disco of colors to shine upon our faces.

We don't even look back at the ship; why should we? Who knows what just happened and why this place is so ruined now. We must get to safety first, in case anyone finds us. How did Ace even get in? No time to think about that right now. Safety is first.

It seems as though the black plains of scorched,

133

ruined land stretches on forever. The smell of burnt meat whisks my nostrils hairs. The sky is quite lovely, in a certain way. It's completely empty, excluding the brain mound in the sky. The lack of stars and color leaves the view above looking like an empty void as if we are in the middle of nowhere in space.

The ground is slightly wet, my feet clomping against the dirt as we stumble through. In the back of my ears, I hear some sort of noise. It's coming from my left, and it is very faint.

Tick.

"...uld we use any of the fleshy material we found in the study rooms?" a feminine voice asks. I can't tell where this one is coming from.

Tick.

I look around for some sort of hiding spot, and my eyes land on a few bumps in the land and some large rocks. That's the perfect spot.

Tick.

"We need to hide behind those rocks," I say to Mic, pointing forward. He briefly glances at them before nodding his head and waddling along. I sneak behind him, and we climb over the light gray, jagged as a knife rocks and position our backs right up against them.

Tick.

"We don't know what DNA they contain," another voice says, this one coarse and rough. A dried-out voice, one lacking water. "It is too risky. We already have the perfect specimen."

Tick.

The sound of footsteps rings in my ears as I can see their shadow protruding over the rock and past my outstretched legs.

Tick.

"Seems we have also found a crash site," the empty voice says. "That's the first of three."

Tick.

Three crash sites? We were one…Ace was another.

Tick.

So who's the third?

"Tick," I say. What? Why did I just say that out loud?

"There wasn't a tick that time," Mic quietly whispers. "It's the clock tower. I thought I knew that sound…."

"Why didn't it tick again?" I ask.

Crunch.

More footsteps? It doesn't sound like the two from before. I turn around and slowly peek my head over the rock to see a teal-skinned man with five arms and a ragged pink cloth over his chest, as well as a peach-colored being with remains of crusty seagrass-green shell dotting his body. Haven't I seen him before?

"Excuse me? You look very familiar," I whisper to them as I climb over the rock.

"Seventh?" Mic asks from behind me. The two

135

figures turn to us as the silence is broken by The Seventh's words.

"We're all going to die soon."

"Obvious enough pal," Mic says. He walks past me over to The Seventh, where they share an enormous hug. "Haven't seen you in a while. You look horrible."

The Seventh lets out a meaty laugh.

"Don't even get me started," he jokes. "The places I've been and the things I've seen have scarred me."

"You and me both, brother," Mic says. "So, where to?"

"We must find some sort of shelter," the teal man says. He points up to the brain, which gets closer and closer. "Does anyone know the planet we are on?"

"It's called the Valley," Mic says. "It's an Astrual Ring planet."

The teal man raises one finger to his red dome helmet, where he taps the antennae on the side. His thin green visor pulses with a lighter shade, and a hologram spurts out. A glitchy, 32-bit rendition of the Valley lights up from the visor, and the planet's shape slowly spins around.

"Is this it?" the teal man asks. Mic walks toward the hologram, holding his hands up to it. The light from his visor brightens the area around us and gives color to the monochrome land.

"This…is this a live scan?" he asks.

"Yes," the teal man responds. "That brain in the

136

sky is my home, and I'm able to connect to a camera upon it."

"No…," Mic drones. "Look at it. It's all charred…my home."

I walk around the hologram to see the other side of the planet, and it shows a large chunk has been taken out. Mic's skin erupts in goosebumps as he grabs onto his perfectly combed hair. He pulls it down, ripping a few strands from his scalp.

"Right there," The Seventh says, pointing to a blinking spot on the hologram. "That's us and…."

He points to a spot right above us.

"There's some ruined buildings. It might be useful until we figure out where to go."

~~

Inside the monster mine, Magona stands before the tube filled with the body of Al-X. He places his only hand on the glass, rubbing it up and down. His bladed arm swings around as if being played with by the wind.

"He's beautiful," Magona cries. "Who else has seen such a specimen?"

"No one, my lord," Sergeant Airn says, kneeling beside Magona. Magona's purple robes glisten and shine in the lab's white lighting. "Only you."

"Good…good, I'm glad you think so. Once we perform the blood transfusion into this perfect body, we can hope that The Seventh makes his way here."

"Are you sure he is still alive, my lord?"

"Do you doubt me? He is a GOD!" Magona yells. He slams a fist on the tube and a small crack forms in the glass. He quickly turns his head toward Airn, and she looks upon his wrinkled, dried-out face and his deep, empty white eyes. They look more like molding milk than actual eyeballs. "WE ARE NOT SO EASILY KILLED!"

"I am sorry, my lord," Airn quickly apologizes, bowing her head. "I misspoke my reflection, and I do take back what I said."

"Good," Magona says, his desert of a mouth still gaping open. The teeth he has left crumble with every breath, and his gums pulse with black veins and protrude from his skin-wrapped bones. "Now, go pull the lever and lower the subject in."

Airn nods her head and rises to her feet. She walks over to a control panel on the opposite side of the wall. A slanted desk covered in buttons and switches, she's only concerned with the large, extruding lever in the wall with a silver shaft and a bright red ball at the top.

"I shall enter myself," Magona says. "Once the hatch is closed, begin."

Magona walks to the second tube next to Al-X's and opens a small hatch at the base. He crawls on his scrawny hand and bony knees into the tube, where the heavy mechanical hatch slams shut behind him. He places his hand against the clear glass tube, leaving fingerprints and blood on the window. The tube is empty beside Magona.

138

"Start," Magona mouths from inside. Airn nods and puts both hands on the lever, struggling to pull it down. She jumps up a few times to try and put weight on it, but when she does, it immediately slams down, and she crashes to the floor, face first.

In Magona's tube, a panel in the top slides open, and a robotic arm glides down. At the end of it, it holds a small needle. Magona raises his bladed arm up, and his purple sleeve drops down, revealing his charred and warped skin. Veins pulse with an orange glow and the shredded skin and muscles contort as the blade shines brighter and brighter.

The arm grows closer to Magona and inches the needle toward one large vein near Magona's shoulder. Airn waits momentarily, and the arm quickly shoves the needle into Magona. Orange goo slides through the needle and travels through a muddy plastic tube connected to the back. He doesn't flinch nor even make a movement. He's as still as a stone.

All of the dingy tubes connected to the floating Al-X body flow with the orange liquids. It trickles into the unliving body, and his stitched-together skin throbs with light and movement, and his eyes blast open. Totally black eyes, with a red slit iris. His eyebrows bend downward, and a broken smile forms on his face.

His yellowed, chipped teeth outline his black gums and lips. Bubbles form in the green liquid from his mouth, and his angled cheekbones move up, causing his face to appear more demonic. The tips of his ears melt from the bottom up, and the liquified skin slithers through the patches of curly black hair onto his forehead, where two holes open up, and two bones slide out about five inches into the air. The gooey skin wraps around the bones, bending up at the top. They appear to have the look of horns, as if from a devil.

In the other tube, Magona stands motionless. His body has been completely flushed of all color, even in his veins. They do not flow any more, and even his eyes aren't the usual cloudy color. They're pitch black, a void. His face has the outline of a skull, and the skin begins to flake off. His yellow skeleton shines through, and his purple robe slides off his body.

Airn lays her eyes upon the nude body of Magona, a genital-less husk of a being with no internal organs left beside a still beating heart, whose arteries wrap around the ribs that begin to show. Skin particles glide to the ground as the mechanical arm finally pulls the needle from the arm. Magona's lifeless body falls to the ground, and Airn hears a loud crash and a shatter right after.

She runs over to the tube and pulls open the hatch. It's definitely a heavy door, but she manages. She crouches down and looks into the tube, where Magona's skeleton lays on the ground; some ribs and the skull shattered into a million jagged pieces. Even the heart is gone. Skin flakes dot the floor like fallen snow, and Magona's purple robe covers his scrawny ass.

140

"My lord?"

No response.

"Was this supposed to happen?"

Airn stumbles backward, thinking about the dead Magona before her. What happened? Where is Magona? Is he inside Al-X? She looks over at the hulking beast, and he slams both of his meaty arms into the glass, and nothing happens but a thud. Airn stays frozen in place. He does it again; nothing. Again, nothing. Again, something. The glass cracks just a tiny bit, as small as the fracture Magona caused earlier. Airn decides not to stay down in the lab any longer, and she runs toward the stairs, up to the surface.

~~

"Wow," I say. The view is…distracting.

I stand amongst the other three at the top of the broken clock tower, watching the inferno rage on. The gray stone base continues to dance around with the lime green flames, which have overtaken the whole first level of the building. Windows are shattered, and infrastructure is revealed.,

The Seventh sits against one of the fallen cogs, one that's size is almost double anyone here. Mic stands in the far corner of the clock tower, where the angled wall has been completely torn away, and he dangles his feet over the edge as he holds onto a piece of rebar. He rests his head against it, and his arms fall to his side. The teal man, who is The Eternal Brian, watches through a hole in the ceiling. He stares at the view of The Eternal Brain, which

141

is his home.

"Is this it?" Mic asks.

"The Eternal Brain is cracking," Brian explains. "If it explodes, it'll suck the entire universe into itself. Same with every other universe. The brain is a gateway, you see. To any galaxy or universe I want. My goal was to look after it; to monitor the energy levels. If the level gets too high, the brain will crack. This universe's levels certainly gained a height I didn't like."

"You set out to find the source and then you found me," The Seventh chimes in. "I had high energy, how come I didn't set off the alarms immediately?"

"Each universe is at its own level. None are the same," Brian explains. "It's when the level drastically increases or decreases that I get involved. The brain is powered by energy from around it. Too much energy…and it's overloaded."

"Like how it is now?" I ask. Brian nods his head.

"Any of y'all have a dying wish?" Mic asks. The green flames reflect off his body, blocking the light from illuminating the rest of the room. "Be as fucking stupid as you want."

"I think we all have a serious answer as well as a joke answer, pal," The Seventh laughs. "But my shitty one would be…lemme think. Maybe to go on a nice relaxing vacation on some Cosmo-Edge Ring planet."

"You think the Cosmo-Edge people allow outsiders? They have so many sticks up their asses, they're basically a stick sharpener," Mic jokes. We all let out a slight chuckle.

"What about you, Janx?" Mic asks me. I laugh and try to think of something stupid.

"Well…," I begin. "I've always wanted to garden. I want to be on some peaceful countryside where I just tend to some plants and sell them."

"That's nice," The Seventh nods.

"Yeah," Brian agrees.

"You next," I say, pointing to Brian. He sighs before the wrinkles on his face mold into a smile.

"I'd love to one day be able to use The Eternal Brain to move freely from one universe to another," he explains. "I could meet the one for me. I could find my family again. It would be amazing."

"How long have you been stuck in that brain?" I ask.

"Forever. I had a family at some point. They were made alongside me…," Brian says. His voice slowly grows melancholy. "But that's besides the point. Mr. Seven, you can go next."

"Aw, shucks," The Seventh says. "If I had a GOOD dying wish, like a true warrior wish, I'd want to go out in a blaze of glory. I'd want to tear my enemy apart as flames bellow around me. I'd want to kill Magona that way."

"Have any of these been your funny answers?" Mic asks. "These all seem like…really personal."

143

"What do you mean, Mr. Vacation Man?" Brian jokingly asks. Mic looks at him annoyingly, but the three of us burst out laughing. "You don't want to go to a nice beach deep down?"

Mic turns his head back to the base, where the green inferno shows no signs of stopping. The laughter turns to silence, an awkward kind. It just feels empty again. Besides the soft lime glow, the rest of the clock tower's walls remain dark and gray.

"Do you hear that?" Brian whispers. The Seventh and I perk our heads up, and Mic looks back. Brian quietly drops to the ground and places the side of his head against the wood. A light shines up from the spiral staircase in the middle of the room.

"Shit," I say.

"Shit," The Seventh says.

"Shit," Brian says.

"Shit," Mic says.

A head pokes out from the stairs. Brian grabs onto it with three of his arms and pulls the person up. They let out a womanly scream as Brian squeezes her in his arms.

"Who are you!" Brian yells out.

"You should've killed me when you had the chance," she says. Mic steps out of view of the base, and the green light shines upon her face.

Airn's face.

~The Purpose~

"Let me go!" Airn yells out.

"Good luck with that," Brian yells as he restrains Airn, who tries to free herself.

"He'll be free to kill you ANY moment now," Airn yells through clenched teeth. The area around her black eyes bleeds with dark blood.

"Who?" The Seventh asks. He stands up from the cog he sat upon and walks over to Airn. He stops right before her feet. Airn laughs in his face; spit droplets land on his peach skin.

"My lord, Magona," she growls. The Seventh stumbles backward.

"He's dead," The Seventh says. "He's been dead."

"On the contrary, pest," a demonic voice echoes around the clock tower. We all look around to see where the source is, but Brian lets his guard down for a moment, and Airn breaks free. She turns around and grabs onto two of Brian's arms, snapping them backward. The cracking sounds match the sight of bones breaking his teal skin.

The green visor on his helmet pulses with light as a sound grows louder and louder. The ruby-red blood pours out as he screams at the top of his lungs. He shoves his fingers on his other three hands into Airn's sides, and they pierce her skin. She screams and pushes Brian's arms further back.

Vroom.

Vroom.

Vroom.

Vroom.

SHBROOOOOOM.

A beam of green light explodes from his helmet, puncturing Airn's face. Sparkles of lightning shock outwards from the beam, crackling around the room and leaving burn marks wherever they hit. Mic, The Seventh, and I all crouch down to avoid the blast. I close my eyes briefly and bow down to the ground as the light gets brighter and bright, and Brian's screams grow louder and louder.

The screams continue, bursting my eardrums until...everything goes dark, and the screaming stops. The only sound besides the extreme ringing is the sound of a body dropping. I quickly open my eyes, and they adjust to the intense darkness. I look up to Brian, whose two broken arms fall to his side. He holds up his three remaining hands, and they are drenched in blood. Veins bulge from his skin as he quickly breathes in and out.

At his feet, Airn's body lay lifeless. Her neck ends in a charred stump of disintegrated skin. Her body is ghostly pale, or at least what's left of it. Brian drops to his knees and grabs onto his helmet; the blood-staining handprints on the already red metal. He rips the bowl off his head, and it scrapes the sides of his head, leaving pink cuts. He tosses the helmet away, where it lands next to one of the cogs. The Seventh looks over at Brian and kicks the helmet away further.

"I didn't want to do that…," Brian groans. "I…killed her."

We all ignore him as we look at the top of his face. He has no hair, and the top of his head is entirely smooth, opposite his mouth. Above his wrinkled mouth area, three thin eyes line where the visor was covering. The eyelids slide open and close as thick yellow liquid pools from his purple irises.

"It was for the best, wasn't it?" Brian says. We all snap back into reality as we glare upon the fallen Airn.

"How'd you do that?" I ask.

"Self defense measures," he responds. "Extreme measures."

"Good…," the demonic voice from before calls out. "She was a liability anyways."

In the middle of the room, a cloud of black smoke begins to form, and the smaller cogs and detritus around the room slightly shudder. Gusts of cold wind blow around us, and I feel goosebumps form on my skin.

"What pleasant surprise," the voice says. Starting from the floor, a figure forms from the black smoke. White foot and leg bones of a human skeleton are created first. Following that, the pelvic area and lower stomach are shaped of the dark mist, and they support the top half's black ribs streaked with glowing ruby red cracks. Its arms are formed next, and they're white, elongated bones with

147

the tip of the fingers reaching past the knees. However, its right arm ends in a sharp blade made of the black mist.

Lastly, its head is whipped together and takes the form of a smooth white skeleton with one empty eye socket and one shining red eye. The jaw is soft, and the mouth looks welded shut. Despite that, he manages to speak.

"Hello, The Seventh," he says. The Seventh's eyes open wide, and he gasps loudly. He takes a step backward, almost tripping over a bent plank.

"Y-you…it can't be," he stutters. "I killed you, I know I did."

"You really didn't know I came back?" Magona laughs. "Or did you know and in your mind you just kept denying it…."

Magona takes a step closer to The Seventh, who stands frozen in shock. His ghostly figure circles the peach God, placing his skeletal hand on The Seventh's shoulder. The Seventh's eyes stay frozen as Magona raises his blade. He rubs the end of it against the side of The Seventh, lights enough to not draw blood.

"Let him go," Mic yells out. Magona turns his smooth head to look straight at Mic. His singular red eye rotates and moves back and forth, focusing on the studiously dressed man.

"I can let him go, but I'll have to kill the three of you. You only told me to release him…," Magona says. Mic's face turns to an angered expression, and he stands his ground as Magona intimidates him. "And besides... isn't killing him setting him free?"

I look at Mic's eyes and can tell precisely what he will do. I then look at Brian, who nods at me. We need to defuse this, not make it worse.

"You can have me, just let him go," Mic yells. Magona laughs.

"Sounds like a plan," Magona scoffs.

"What?" Mic asks as Magona's lean body whisks forward with a puff of black smoke. It fills the entire room, and I try to waft it away. I have to close my eyes; it hurts so much. This isn't regular smoke; it's like I can hear it breathing.

"You offered," Magona's voice says through the cloud. It begins to clear, and my eyes are set on Mic. He holds onto the blade of Magona, whose arm is lodged into the middle of Mic's chest. The blood dripping out is frozen in time, and so is Mic. Am I just stuck in time? I look down at my dirty, dry fingers and can move them. I turn back up to see Magona's face staring right at me. He rips the blade from Mic's body, and he returns to life. His body slams onto the ground, and all the frozen blood squirts out. It phases through the cloudy body of Magona.

"Hello, girly," Magona says. He takes one step forward, and The Eternal Brian jumps before me. He raises his three unbroken arms to block me from Magona and turns to look at The Seventh, who is still in shock.

"SEV!" he yells. The noise shocks The Seventh's ears, and he blinks a few times before seeing Brian motion with his head to come here. Magona's mouth droops, and his red eye turns right to The Seventh.

"I've killed you before," The Seventh commands. He walks over to join Brian to stand before me as Magona watches in spite. "And I'm certain I can fucking kill you again."

"You can try, but you're talking to the double undead God," Magona scoffs.

"Revenge is the biggest motivation a being can have," The Seventh says as he smiles at Brian. They both nod to each other as they crouch over. "Let's fly."

They both push off the creaky floor forward, running at Magona, who steps backward and raises his sword. He keeps switching between looking at Brian and The Seventh and attempts to slice at them both, to no avail. The two runners jump forward, grabbing onto Magona's arms as they fall forward through one of the weak walls of the clock tower. I run ahead, stopping at the edge of the floor to watch the three of them zoom back up.

Magona blasts through the air with a stream of black fog following behind as The Seventh and Brian hold onto his arms. I can hear their screams as Magona circles the fiery green base, the charred dirt, and dead trees, the dried-up rivers, and the generally open world. All of the landmarks, such as the bridges and houses, are either entirely gone or crumbled. I guess I haven't seen the

Valley how it is now. I'm surprised I haven't noticed it before.

Or at least what's left of it.

"Look at me, Janx," Mic says. I quickly turn to see Mic's body lying against the splintering wall. He holds onto his bleeding chest with both hands. The red wounds stain his fingers and palms and dry up on his pale skin. I can see the blue veins dotted around his body. His suit is ruined now, not that he'd be able to wear it again.

"I see you, Mic," Janx says. "I'm sorry."

"I hear that all the time," Mic laughs. "I guess one more time couldn't hurt."

He slowly places one hand on the ground to try and push himself up more, but he winces as he tries. I grab his arm, putting it back and patting his bloody hands. I can feel the pressure on his chest slowly lower. The color in his eyes turns to a slight gray-blue.

"I'm dying a happy, complete man. Honestly, I am," Mic explains. "I've been waiting for this moment for a long time. Janx, can you promise me something?"

"Anything."

"Make sure Death doesn't carry me away. Not even because I don't want to continue living anymore…but because I couldn't bear to die knowing how he'll feel."
"I'll make sure he knows you died protecting us," I say. Mic shakes his head. His eyes lower; his gaze wanders into the distant space behind me. "No?"

"Let him know I died slowing down Magona," he says. "A hero's death. Like The Seventh mentioned. And remember, you're still alive for a reason."

"I will," I say. I wait for a response, but Mic's veins cease to move. He sits still. I raise my arms up and close his eyelids, waiting for the arrival of Death. But this time, he doesn't show. I lower my body and join him, sitting against the wall. I turn my head to see where Magona is and see the black mist fly straight down from the sky.

I tilt my head as it crashes straight through a patch of overgrown grass on an island in the middle of a small empty pond. It's connected to the mainland by a singular rickety drawbridge. Did they crash into the land? I get back up, trying to adjust my eyes as the smoke from the impact clears. When it does, I see a perfectly square opening in the ground along with a white hatch door angled open next to it.

Where does that lead?

~The 7/2~

"Ah…fuck…," The Seventh groans, feeling the pain of falling down almost three miles down of stairs. He slowly gets himself to his feet as he brushes off the bruises. He's got plenty of blood pouring from multiple open wounds, but he doesn't mind. He's gone long enough without bleeding. At least he knows he's still alive.

Looking around the room, he finds himself in some sort of lobby area. Dirty white walls with yellow markings and light blue designs are lined with molding bright red leather couches, dead decorative plants, and piles of dust. In the panel-lined ceiling, dusty ventilation shafts echo with the distant sounds of unintelligible noises.

He looks forward, away from the stairs, to a dark, foreboding hallway. The floor creaks as if it was made of wood as The Seventh steps on it. The only light source is a singular flickering fluorescent yellow light hanging down by a wire in the middle of the room. Furniture and spare clothes are strewn across the entire room.

"Are we going in?" Brian asks from behind. The Seventh screams and jumps away as he sees Brian half bent over, holding onto his broken elbows. The red-stained bones stick out of his teal skin into jagged, cracked ends. The area around the punctures is covered in dried and wet red blood.

"Are you ok? Do you need any help?" The Seventh asks. He tries to touch Brian's wounds, but he backs away.

153

"We just need to get out of here," Brian responds. He looks around the room as he walks toward the dark hallway. "There may be an easier escape than walking up those stairs again."

"You want to go deeper?" The Seventh asks.

"It couldn't hurt," Brian responds.

—

"Are you there?" Death asks.

The crystals are black and colorless. The shines are gone; the jagged hallways crack with the passage of time. Death walks through Meiv's home, her crystal of space. This time, she is gone. She died long ago.

Death knows that, but he still checks from time to time. It has been countless sun rotations since Magona ravaged the universe. Only a few places remain, such as this. The Valley still stands as well, although it is now closer to The Eternal Brain than ever before. Death knows that.

Death also knows that the only four that could stop Magona are gone. Nobody has seen them in a long time. Planets have died, and species have ceased. Death has been trying to track them down to no avail. Just standing in the broken, empty home of Meiv is hard enough for Death.

He can feel how many lives still remain. It's only two. Magona and Airn. Is there a point for Death to even continue in this realm? Should he just go kill Magona? Can he?

He suddenly feels a change. He feels more alive. Four more. Could it be? Death looks around the dark home one last time before he is dragged by an invisible force to the Valley. He knows what this means. Someone is dead.

—

Brian and The Seventh walk into a large, clean laboratory room. It's a substantially large and brightly lit room compared to the tight, dark, claustrophobic hallways they walked through. Two tubes reach from the floor to almost the top of the ceiling. One of the tubes is cracked open, with the glass spread across the floor, and the room is flooded with some sort of green liquid. It reaches up around a foot from the ground.

The Seventh notices the liquid came from the tube on the left, and he notes it in his head. The Seventh and Brian walk into the room via the staircase down, and they both notice the gargantuan dirty footsteps leading up the steps.

"A giant?" Brian asks.

"I don't think I want to know," The Seventh responds. They both stand on the lowest dry stair before slowly lowering their legs into the mysterious flowing green flood. It's warm. Around the room, paintings of scientists and computers line the walls, as well as debris and shards of glass floating amongst the liquid.

"Is there a drain somewhere?" The Seventh asks.

"I'll go check the button machines," Brain answers. He wafts through the flood to a yellow panel on the wall with a multitude of red and blue buttons and levers. "Hm."

Brian places a finger on his chin and taps away. He analyzes the buttons closely, looking at the chipped labels on each one. After a minute of thinking, he presses the top most blue button. The white light in the room turns off with a groan, and a dim red light flips on instead.

"Not that one," he says. He presses another, and a loud suction noise echoes through the room. The flood slowly drains into a filter in the middle of the room, and The Seventh shakes his legs to dry off. "That one."

The Seventh approaches both tubes, looking at each one. Brian decides to check out the framed photos. Some are of human scientists, while others are of flaming Formes. Each picture has a name at the bottom, and the largest one says:

'HEAD SCIENTIST OF THE BLOOD TRANSFUSION WING — Dr. AIRN DOLOS'

Another reads:

'LEADING MEMBER OF THE WRENCH THEORY — Dr. ATHENA PRILLAMAN'

Such interesting people. The painting of Athena Prillaman displays an older woman with short black hair and a mechanical silver gas mask covering her mouth. She wears a white lab coat dotted with dried brown blood and leathery blue gloves. In one of her hands, she holds a rusty hacksaw over her shoulder. Cute.

In Airn Dolos' photo, it's the face of Sergeant Airn, but younger and less evil. Long black hair with streaks of lime green flow down her clean white lab coat. She stands up straight with her hands held behind her. Her smooth face is wrinkled by her joyful smile, and her pure purple eyes add some color to the otherwise drab paintings.

Still examining them closely, The Seventh opens a hatch on the right tube. He peeks his head inside and sees some sort of skeleton lying on the ground. Its face is long and stretched down. The ribcage is all disproportionate, and the ribs bend and angle in all directions, some longer than others. The eye cavities bleed into where the nose should be, and all the holes melt in either direction. The lower jaw hangs open with a loose connection to the skull, and sharp metal sticks poke from inside the mouth, acting as teeth.,

Its split-in-half spinal cord ends in the pelvic bone, which ends in nothing. There are no leg bones. Both arms stop at the elbow joint on either side of the body. However, a dull, silver blade has been shoved in the right arm between the humerus. Barbed wire wraps around the collarbones and neck, and two pipes connect the shoulders to the elongated face. One singular horn sticks out from the left side of the skull.

"What is this place?" The Seventh asks, pulling his head back out and slamming the hatch closed. "And where did Magona go?"

"I'm not sure. But we've been walking for a while, do you think we should just try to use the stairs?" Brian suggests.

"At this point, it'll take less time to walk up there then it would to find another exit so let's go," The Seventh says. They both walk up the stairs into the dark hallway they came from as an animalistic scream shakes the walls. "Which way did that come from?"

They look both ways: toward the stairs and in the opposite direction. No sign of life can be seen either way.

"Is it Magona?" Brian asks.

After a few more seconds of looking, they both turn in the opposite direction of the stairs. Something is walking toward them; they can hear the slight footsteps. Is it Magona? Or something else entirely?

They both stare as Brian pulls something from underneath his pink cloth. He holds some sort of metallic green oval object, which he twists in half and throws down the hallway. It emits a soft green light as it bounces along the limestone floors and passes something, illuminating it momentarily. Not a skinny Magona-like figure, but a large, chubby head. We're talking about the size of the hallway, which is already big as is.

"What…is that?" Brian asks. He leans in one step forward, trying to see it better. As he does, the face reveals

158

itself from the darkness by moving into the light emitting from the lab we just exited. Black eyes, with red slit irises. Sweaty, grease-covered skin that is dotted with patches of dandruff-filled black hair. Cuts and wounds dragging through every inch of the face held together by multiple stitches and staples. Its mouth hangs open, and the slobbery, yellow tooth face growls as it continues to move forward.

"Let's get to those stairs!" The Seventh yells. He and Brian turn and push off the slippery ground. They both stumble forward before catching their balance and blasting along. Their feet slap against the limestone floor, creating wet sounds as they run.

They pass by openings in the walls to other dark rooms and hallways, and they dodge fat, hairy arms coming out of each one, trying to grab the duo. They begin to breathe harder as they run. The white lights of the hallway start to flicker on as the black mist from before circles before them.

The Seventh and Brian look around at their surroundings; the newly revealed white walls with blue, red, and yellow lines are painted around them. The fog molds into Magona again, and he flies backward at the same pace the duo runs forward.

"I'd like you to meet my creation; one half me…the other half me as well!" he boasts. "The blood of my physical body, as well as the body of one of my blood creations. I call him…the Seventh Hunter. Quite poetic."

159

"Let us go, Magona! Or just kill us now!" The Seventh yells.

"Oh, you'll all die alright. Just not now," Magona laughs. He quickly speeds up, as does the hunter. The arms continue to appear out of every opening they pass by, much to their confusion. It defies all laws of anything. In the far distance, they can finally see the natural light coming down from the top of the stairs.

"We're almost th-," Brian starts. He's cut off as one of the hands launches out and slams him into the wall. The Seventh hears a few crunches as he compresses the painted bricks. He falls to the ground, and The Seventh quickly slows down.

"Brian?" The Seventh calls out.

"Go…on without…me," Brian says from the floor. The Seventh sees a dent in the side of his head. His skull is broken and is probably piercing through his brain.

"Not happening."

The Seventh crouches down as the stomps of the hunter grow louder. He pulls one of Brian's arms over his shoulder and struggles to pick him up. The Seventh prevails, however, and he begins to run against with Brian slowly recuperating next to him.

"Why…are you bringing me? I'm slowing…you down," he says. The Seventh doesn't give an answer. He just keeps running, running toward the light. Eventually, Brian is able to get back on his feet. He stumbles at first as The Seventh lets go, but they continue to dodge the hands and quick punches as they run into the lobby from before. They both stop at the bottom of the stairs, looking back as the hunter crawls toward them. The Seventh takes one last look at the broken furniture, dead plants, and peeling paint as he takes one step on the staircase.

"Brian?" The Seventh asks.

"Yes?" Brian asks back.

"We're almost free," The Seventh answers. "Let's finish this, yeah?"

"Yeah," Brian says. The Seventh smiles and nods his head as he begins up the stairs. Brian looks at his two broken arms; the punctured skin is still bleeding. He feels the side of his, where the dent feels fleshy and rough in different areas. He probably won't make it long; his brain is already damaged. Any more, and he will be a walking corpse. He needs to make a choice, and he needs to make it soon.

—

"You know what I told you," someone says. Death looks down to discover he is now in a broken clock tower, surrounded by gears and fallen wood planks. He also sees Mic lying on the ground beside him, blood pooling from his mouth and around his chest.

"Mic," Death calls out, kneeling down to his level. Mic's eyelids shake as they try to close, but Mic continues to hold onto life. He raises a shaky, bloody hand up and places it on Death's yellow patella. "What happened?"

"Did you come for me?" Mic asks. "Or her?"

161

He points to behind me, where Death looks to see a headless body lying near the stairs. The neck has been cauterized by an unknown force. Death turns back to Mic, who now has one eye fully closed. His lips are covered in blood, dripping from the corners of his mouth.

"You can take her, but not-," Mic coughs up some blood, which splatters onto Death's legs. "Me. I have served my purpose. I have no wish to continue to exist. Let me rot. Please. I have aided countless generations, and now that we're the last…I have no one else to love. Let me go, and please let the others live. They're our only hope."

"I know," Death says. He watches as Mic flashes a quick, weak smile as his other eye closes. Mic's body slowly fades away before Death's black eyes, and Death looks away. Nearby, another death catches Death's senses. The last few droplets of blood drip onto the floor and Mic's soul is erased from existence.

—

"SEV!" Brian yells out from behind. The Seventh stops right at the top of the staircase. They are so close to escaping. He turns around to see Brian standing a few steps down. "Go."

"Not without you," The Seventh pleads. "Let's go, we can shut him in here!"

"Have you seen the thing?" Brian asks with a slight chuckle. "It'll break through the door immediately. I'll stay behind and act as a rock."

"A rock?" The Seventh cries out. "Come on Brian, we're already close enough to escape and find Janx and leave!"

"No," Brian says in a cold voice. "Close the door, Sev."

"I can't."

"Close it now. Save yourself. Do you see how injured I am?"

"You can still make it," The Seventh yells to Brian.

"He's already here," Brian says just as an arm reaches out from the darkness behind him. The hunter's greasy, thick-fingered hand erupts from the shadows and grabs onto the body of Brian. He doesn't look back; he just stands there.

"BRIAN!" The Seventh yells out.

"Close the door," Brian says calmly. "Now."

The Seventh pauses momentarily and then looks at the open hatch on his left. The heavy white door made of the richest steel shines with the brain's white light above. It seems as though the universe is telling The Seventh to close it. He takes one last look at Brian, who smiles as the muddy, chubby face of the hunter slowly reveals itself. Its square teeth spin and crack open to form sharper, triangular teeth as its mouth cracks open wide.

"Find Janx."

The Seventh grabs onto the other end of the four-foot wide hatch, pulling with all his might. His muscles grow, and his veins bulge, blood flowing rapidly through

163

him. The hatch groans as it's closed, and The Seventh looks down the dark stairs as The Eternal Brian closes his three eyes, and the hunter throws him into his seemingly endless dark red mouth. The hunter's eyes lock with The Seventh's as the hunter crunches and the hatch slams shut. Some mechanical noises emit from the hatch, but The Seventh doesn't stay long to hear them. He turns around and wipes water from his eye as he runs across the black hills.

His only goal? To find Janx and escape the Valley.

—

"Are you Death?" Brian asks.

"Yes."

Death stands before Brian, who was spat out by the hunter right after the hatch was closed. The staircase is entirely dark, but the lighting from outside slightly illuminates Death's outline.

"I hope my sacrifice was worth it," Brian says. He rests the side of his head on the wall behind him, facing toward the light. He looks up at the highly close brain in the sky, growing ever closer. Brian's body is crushed and beaten; his bones broken and cracked, and his muscles shredded and torn. Blood streams down from every hole, and none of his limbs are responsive. "My home looks good up close. Shame it has to blow the fuck up."

He lets out a weak laugh, followed by coughs and blood squirting out.

"Should I have stayed? It probably would've happened either way, but I could've brought an army. A large group from another universe. Maybe our enemies are our allies somewhere else among the stars."

"You did great," Death chimes in.

"I could do better," Brian finally lets out. His eyes shut for good, and his head bounces down a little. Death turns to the fiery base, where the green light mixes with the brain's white glow.

—

The Seventh reaches the bottom of the base, opposite the clock tower side. He finds a rusty, half-broken ladder leading to the very top. He runs across the uneven black hills, jumping over small rocks and little dried-up streams. He hears the impending pounds and impacts of the hunter behind him, still trying to exit the lab.

He gets to the ladder, placing his hand on a jagged leg and his left foot on the bottom bar. He tries to climb up, but a hand touches his shoulder. He looks over to see a woman. Black hair; emerald green eyes; a soft, round face; a big but cute nose; thin eyebrows that curve on either end.

"Again?" The Seventh cries out. "I thought you were gone."

"I was, but...," she says. "You're almost at the end of your journey, do you know that? You came a long way from being trapped."

"I can't do anything anymore. I have been running…running ever since I was freed. And now I face this…this HUNTER. Is the hunter the death of me?"

She nods. The Seventh understands. He knows it was only inevitable.

"So then what? I die, and Janx is killed too?" The Seventh asks.

"You must not let her die," she says back. "I know you saw me in her…and it's not a coincidence. You are bound by fate to protect her. Just like you tried to with me. You have run all across the universe…but you continue to run into her."

"What if I fail again?" The Seventh asks.

"The only way you fail is if you don't try."

The Seventh looks back to the lab's entrance, where the hunter flies through the door, cracking it off and slamming into a leafless tree nearby. He looks at his lover…into her eyes one last time before facing what he knows is coming.

"Everyone dies," she says. "This is your chance to make that moment important."

The Seventh nods and looks up at the top of the ladder, where the brain fills the sky. Only a matter of time before it collides with the Valley. Maybe I can escape on the roof? Only one way to find out.

~~

I stumble across the only standing bridge attached to the clock tower, which reaches the top of the burning base. The rickety brown bridge sways in the heavy winds, and I try to hold onto the weathered string handrails as I walk along it. The fire is extremely high at this point. It's almost touching the bottom of the bridge. I must get away from the clock tower…as soon as possible.

I look up at the brain, which almost fills the entire sky. It has already broken the atmosphere. Only a matter of time before it collides with the Valley. Maybe I can find another ship?

"JANX!" The Seventh calls out. I look back at the top of the base before me, where I see him running toward me. He's on the complete other side, about twenty yards away. He's running at full speed toward me, and I squint to see if someone's following him. Odd, nothing is behind him.

That is, until a creature of mass proportion flies into the sky, coming down and stomping on the very edge of the base. A blast of air and dust travels in all directions, stopping before me. It hits The Seventh in the back, and he almost falls, but he uses it to get a speed boost for a second. I take one step onto the stone roof.

"GET OFF!" The Seventh yells out, his voice cracking from the volume.

"I NEED TO HELP YOU!" I yell back. It's just us two left…I don't see Brian. "PLEASE!"

"YOU DON'T UNDERSTAND!" he yells back as the creature waddles behind him. A disproportionate being of immense height, with greasy human skin that's stitched

167

together quite poorly. His arms dangle before him, swinging side to side as he almost jumps forward with each step. The black eyes on the crusty, bloated face spin around like googly eyes. I hear a large crackle and pop below me, and I look down to see the fire has now reached the bridge. Fuck.

"COME ON!" I yell. "THE FIRE IS RISING!"

"GOOD!" The Seventh responds back. "LET IT!"

What is he doing? He's slowing down. Why is he slowing down?

"WHAT ARE YOU DOING?" I yell out.

"SAVING YOUR ASS, JANX!" he yells back. What does THAT mean? I take another step onto the stone, but The Seventh shakes his head. I take a step back, and The Seventh begins to reach within a yard or two of me. He's so close...but so is the monster.

The Seventh reaches the edge of the bridge but comes to a screeching halt. I look at him in his empty eyes. His mouth drips down on either side. I beckon for him to keep walking with my hand.

"It's me he wants," The Seventh says.

"No, you're coming with me, we're going to fix everything!" I yell at him. "Don't you fucking dare try anything stupid I SWEAR!"

"Saving you isn't stupid," The Seventh says. "Besides, if you're still alive now...you have a purpose. Maybe Mic is right about death. You die right after you complete your goals."

"Sev, I swear…," I begin.

"Janx," he says. "This is my final purpose. I always thought you looked like my wife since I saw you after crash landing. Funny how things work out."

I look down to see The Seventh's foot caught underneath one of the wooden panels lining the bridge's bottom. Around us, the flames bellow upward, warping around the bridge, giving us a nice green glow as the monster's thunderous stomps grow closer.

The Seventh smiles. I don't. He flips his foot up, and the panel goes flying. Everything happens in slow motion after. The connections of the bridge burn away, and it begins to fall. I feel it under my own feet, my weight pushing the bridge down even faster. I turn around as I reach a forty-five-degree angle and grab onto the charred wooden panels.

The bridge collapses to the hills, where I slam onto the grass. The opposite side of the bridge, connected to the clock tower, snaps forward. The tower's top half bursts out a dust cloud and the bricks, stones, and gears fall to the ground. The building crumbles and collapses in on itself. It ends in a cloud of dirt.

I roll onto my beaten back, where I watch the base, which used to be gray and stone, now take on a green and fiery appearance. The Seventh stands between two arching flames, where the monster appears behind him. The Seventh looks down at me, and he waves. The monster's grubby hands grab onto him, one on his chest and one on his legs. He's raised into the air, and....

Both sides of The Seventh disappear into the opposing flames; just as they overtake the monster. The building is now completely covered in green. The brain is close now, closer than before. I just lay there; on the ground. Right here. Right, where I have ended up. Maybe Mic WAS right. I must have one last thing to do?

I close my eyes as the white light from the brain envelops the world. The black, charred land, collapsed buildings, and roaring lime base shine white as they are consumed by the light. Me next? I hear a weird, whisking sound coming from next to me. I turn my head to my right, where the dark spirit of Magona can be seen from afar. It soars toward me, but even as it reaches me and holds out its bladed arm, the white light wraps his black smog up.

The brain has collided with the Valley.

~The Goodbye~

Frozen in space.

Forever.

Or at least until I end it all. Which I do have the power to.

Nothing exists outside of a small pocket of...something. No stars, no space, not even any air. It's just Magona, and I left. The universe cannot end until life and Death are broken, and the brain's destruction enabled that to happen. But...my body has already been destroyed. I am an anomaly.

I both exist, but I also don't. Technically, this universe IS gone. So is every single other. We're just in a pocket in the void. But even the void doesn't exist anymore. Everything is nothing. Even when I turn my head away, I still see Magona. I can move around, but he doesn't get any closer or farther.

His body isn't even physically here. Only the memory of it is. That's all we are, just memories. That's what anyone becomes, regardless of who or what they are. Once you're gone, you're just a memory. People can remember you and recall how it felt to be with you, but that's it. A feeling and a memory.

Magona's feeling is dark and cold. His memories cloud the space around me, and I'm reminded of all the people I had to carry away because of him, whether directly or indirectly. Shawn Jr., Mac Marvin, Rink

McNatalie, the man with simply a right hand as an identifiable trait, Chuck Charles.

Owen, Redd, L, and Judith.

Aid, Den, and Cash.

Nolen, Maya Patel, Nexgas, Heaven's Eye, and Box Master, Stephen Ramos.

Matthew.

Janx, Reez, Row-N.

The Eternal Brian.

The demiGods.

The Gods.

I used to write down each person I carried away. I thought it was…fun…for a while. To know the personality of everyone. But that became too much. It didn't even last an ordinary lifetime. It wasn't until recently I began that again. When I had to keep popping up near certain people.

The Valley Forge Force.

L and his group of defenders.

The forgotten triplets.

The heroes.

The Locanagwan three.

And the celestial beings that used to be my allies.

I kept track of them because I knew they would fare against the likes of Magona and his brainwashed army. They were just regular species anyways; no modifications or anything. They were up against how many beings of a higher power? If only the groups could've combined sooner…or even at all. The heroes were all picked off...the triplets and the Valley Forge Force were all cannon fodder. L and his friends and the Locanagwan three fought the most. They succeeded in some parts...but couldn't achieve the end goal.

Do I blame them?

No.

Do I blame myself?

Partially.

I could have stopped Magona from rising, but so could so many others. I used to believe it was clearly only my fault and that I was the only one in the wrong. But everyone was in the evil that day. The day The Seventh was sealed away, and Magona truly began his plan. He knew everything was already going well.

I just...could tell.

Should I destroy this memory? What's the point if I do? No one else is alive. Everythings gone. I can't escape anywhere... I'm in the same state as him. But I am Death..., and I can simply erase his physical memory from this space, and I, too, would be sent away.

I'd be free.

I'd be safe.

I'd be done.

One would think that someone would've been able to kill him for all the wrong he has done. All the people who opposed his plan would've had the right amount of heart to triumph over his evil. Good always wins in the end. At least, it should. But alas, no one ever looks past the happy ending.

For every Gwyn being killed and stopping one of Magona's forces, there's an L dying shortly after and lowering our ally count by one. For every Janx and Reez reunion, there's a history of a troubled past between the two of them and me lurking around the corner. For every... never mind, you get the idea. It seems as though no matter the situation, a dark hope lingers amongst all, living or dead.

What power do I have at this point in time? Does time even exist anymore? I can see but also can't... it's more of a feeling of sight. I still sense Magona and his memories-no. I still feel The Angelic and his memories.

The person that The Angelic was before everything. One equal with the other Gods, including myself. Whatever happened to that man? That being? That soul? How could he have gotten so corrupt?

I am sick of watching him. I cannot do it any longer.

It is not that I am bored...I just... can't look at him anymore. I can't kill him either...that would just free him. He must suffer.

I hope I can see Life again.

Even just one more time.

~The Realm~

White light.

A feeling of warmth.

But also a coldness creeping in.

I open my eyes, yet… they've already been open this whole time. It's so new, yet feels so familiar as well. How long have I been here for?

A void akin to space surrounds me. But space is empty; space is dark.

This space feels full and light.

Heaven? Am I in heaven? I've only heard about it in tall tales, but this does match the description. If it was heaven, I'd be with Reez already.

Am I dead? Am I inside The Eternal Brain? The faint humming sound around me waves up and down in terms of volume as if the space is singing. Looking down, I see myself.

Where'd my clothes go?

My pale skin shines in the sourceless light, to which I cover my breasts and crotch with my arms. I am dead. This must be the Realm of Death; Mic was wrong. It does exist. Is this it, though? I just walk around this void until….

"Janx?" a voice calls out. A familiar voice. A too-familiar voice. I turn around, facing toward a figure. A soft figure. A too-familiar, pale figure.

"Reez?" I ask, the name cracking in the middle. Is that really him?

He stands a few feet away, his dark gray and nougat mixed fur flowing down his body. I lower my arms to my sides, letting them rest. His red-outlined eyes shine as they look upon me. The scar around his right eye glows bright pink.

"I feel the same way as when I first saw you before I really knew who you were. I thought you were the most beautiful girl I'd ever seen. And I still do," Reez says. "I was afraid you wouldn't like me, and that's why I might have been a little distant at first. But now I wish I was more open with you because I felt a love for you that I've never felt for anyone else. You changed my world for the better, and I wish I could've survived so you wouldn't have needed to come here to see me.

I was able to watch over you from time to time, but I could never make myself known. I only had a limited time to be in the realm of the living, and I didn't want to waste it all. You've read everything I wrote...and I just wanted to say thank you. I have gone through so much horror in my lifetime, and only you have been the light at the end of the tunnel."

I run up to him, wrapping my arms around his back like I haven't seen him in forever. Which is kind of true.

"My body has been tortured by many in different ways...but I felt almost at peace when I died. I thought that despite the grief and despair it would cause you...it

176

would be the last time you'd feel that," Reez says, putting his arms around me. I dig my face into his shoulders, where the warmth of his neck heats up my cold body. "I didn't think about the journal and how it would make you feel, honestly, because when I met you I lost memories and feelings of those events. Even when I would be physically hurt or threatened by goons…I would barely feel anything. I just knew you'd be there for me."

I try to hide it as well as I can, but my eyes begin to tear up. My grip on his back tightens. So does his.

"Is it time?" I ask through rivers pouring down my face and closed eyes. I feel Reez laugh without speaking, his body jolting up a few times. He places one hand on my head, softly rubbing my hair as he leans his forehead on mine.

"Yes," he quietly says. I open my watery eyes to see a glowing white figure approaching, seemingly walking on thin air. As she walks closer, and I wipe the tears from my eyes with my arms still around Reez, her form becomes apparent. She blends in with the remaining blinding void, almost like part of it grew into a being.

A pearly white skeleton with bones that sparkle in the undying light. A soft, pastel pink robe around her neck flows down to her ankles. Tribal markings made of glittery sky-blue diamonds dot her face, and her right-hand holds onto a tall, straight staff that's topped with a glass orb. The sphere contains some sort of spinning pink and yellow mix of light that pulses with every step she takes.

"Hello?" I ask out loud. The figure stops near us, only a few steps away. She rests her left hand on her outstretched right arm and bows her head. Reez lets go and stands beside me, holding one hand on my lower back.

"Life is a beautiful, curious thing, is it not?" the skeleton asks. "Although, it is also an evil and wretched concept." her voice is majestic and soft, yet also loud and clear.

"Are you Death?" Reez asks. "I thought you looked different."

"No," she responds. "I am simply Death's own shadow; but also he is my shadow. I am Life. We both were created when the multi-universe was, but I stayed in this realm whilst he remained in the space of the living."

"Life lives in the Realm of Death?" I ask.

"They both need each other to survive. Without life, there is no death. Without death, there is no life," Life responds to me. "And both of you stand before the End."

"What now? We just walk around until something happens?" Reez asks. Life shakes her head and lays her other hand on the staff.

"I split your soul from your physical form. Your bodies will cease, but your person will not," she says. "Are you both free of any distress and unpleasantry within your hearts?"

"Yes," Reez immediately lets out. I, on the other hand, wait a moment before speaking. Am I ready? Is this really it? I've come all this way just for my home to be destroyed and for everyone around me to die. But I'm here with Reez. That's all I wanted since he was killed.

What DOES my heart feel? Happiness? Sadness? A loss of reason? Whatever it may be, I scrap it; throw it to the side. It doesn't matter. What does is where I am now and who I'm with. And I'm with Reez. I'm complete.

"Yes," I finally mutter.

~~

Two souls conjoined into one.

Two hearts finally reunited.

They're carried away into the realm of the dead by Life. She's a beautiful creature. I watch her from afar, never letting her know I've been killed. She only appears when someone comes to terms with their death. How can Death do that? That's what I think to myself.

Isn't it ironic how Life existed in the realm of the dead and I existed in the realm of the living? Is that funny to some? I always wondered why she wasn't one of the seven Gods. How come I was? I think she was always envious.

I don't blame her. I was envious that she had a more straightforward job. She didn't have to carry away the dead. She didn't have to own up to being a God. She didn't have to face the horrors of the living world. She stayed here. Where it's safe.

Where she could see people in their happiest state. Because when someone dies, their body appears here in the condition they were in when they were the most satisfied. Isn't that sweet? I continue to watch Life walk off into the void of the Realm. She seems happy doing it. And they're the last bodies she'll have to carry. It's over.

"You're free," I whisper, hoping she doesn't hear. Her head bows down. She stops walking.

"I'm not free until you are."

What does she mean? She doesn't have to carry me; I'm content staying here.

"Being free means being dead," she continues. "Being gone. I am still here. No more bodies to drag means no point in staying here. The only way I can be free is if we walk together."

"I still have someone to look after," I respond. "I still have my duties."

"Who cares, Death?" Life yells out, turning to me as she places the orb on top of her staff. "It's over. It's you, him, and me. That's it. Make a choice. Come with me and it erases everything, or stay and leave us three to suffer forever."

I think for a moment. I am stuck watching Magona. He is still in the universe, the only thing keeping it together. He's frozen. At this moment, I happen to be as well.

"You've done everything you could," Life says.

"They're waiting for you, ya know," a cheeky, pipsqueak voice calls into my earhole. I look on my right shoulder, where a small white creature sits. Its body is two snowy circles, with a lovely green scarf separating the two.

180

The black, beady eyes stare at me, and the lack of a mouth leaves its expression unknown. "You've been taking ya sweet ol' time dying."

"Who's waiting for me?" I ask. Flaps of white cover the top of his eyes, giving him an annoyed look.

"Your friends, goddammit!" he yells out. "Don't you wanna be with 'em again? The TV, the Dog?"

"It has been quite a long time," I say.

"Then let's go!" Snowman yells, bouncing around my arms. I look at Life, who stares into my black eyes. I realize what I must do. I grab onto Snowman, and he rests in my hands as I walk forward. Holding him in my left, I hold out my right toward Life. She removes one hand from her staff and grabs onto mine. Together, the three of us walk into the light, into the whiteness of the void. We are no longer trapped. We are free.

Free in the soul oasis of the Realm of Death.

~The Creature Log~

-Dated: 2041

• Arachnavoids

-Species that have human-like builds, with two large eyes and six smaller ones. Their skin can be gray, brown, black, or white and they grow little hairs that protect them from harmful weather conditions. Two sharp fangs hang on either side of their mouth. Arachnavoids have the ability to grow human hair, in any way or style they want.

-Usual Height: 5-6 Feet Tall
-Usual Weight: 120-135 Pounds
-Danger Level: Low
-Place of Origin: Loca
-Cross-Breed: Yes

• Arma-Human

-Normal humans with varying degrees of yellow skin, due to a condition in which too much bilirubin is created from their blood cells mutating from the Locanagwan water.

-Usual Height: 6-7.5 Feet Tall
-Usual Weight: 140-165 Pounds
-Danger Level: Moderately Low
-Place of Origin: Earth II
-Cross-Breed: Yes

● Ascended Guards

-Large wooden skeletons that connect with the darkest
depths of the fiery pits of the universe. Black bones drip
lava onto the ground, past their floating upper bodies.
Their bodies are very sharp, due to their higher status as
the guards of The Divine's pit.
-Usual Height: 8 Feet Tall
-Usual Weight: 400 Pounds
-Danger Level: Moderate
-Place of Origin: Magona
-Cross-Breed: No

● Ascended Priest

-A bony creature of unknown origin. Formed from the four
Ascended Guards of Loca during the confrontation with
Al-X. He wears an inverted white metal suit that covers his
red bones. Spikes adorn his shoulders, and his face is
usually seen covered in blood and decorated with mounds
of flesh.
-Usual Height: 8.5 Feet Tall
-Usual Weight: Unknown
-Danger Level: Extremely High
-Place of Origin: Loca
-Cross-Breed: No

• Ascending Guards

-Large wooden skeletons that connect with nature in order
to live. They serve under the Temple of Akur on each
planet; serving as the base-line guards. They wear white
and purple cloth over their frames. Usually adorned with
plants.
-Usual Height: 8 Feet Tall
-Usual Weight: 320 Pounds
-Danger Level: Extremely Low
-Place of Origin: Magona
-Cross-Breed: No

• Barbarians

-Warriors from a forgotten time. They waltz around in
small clothing, usually only sporting a few pieces of fabric
over their goods. Barbarians are known for their heavy
muscles, extensive egos, and overgrown hair.
-Usual Height: 6-7 Feet Tall
-Usual Weight: 130-165 Pounds
-Danger Level: Moderate
-Place of Origin: Vhorlarx
-Cross-Breed: No

• Bo-Telail

-Underwater medics bred to care for each other, since they
usually live alone. Their brain is surrounded by an almost

translucent chamber of steel, that sits in the top of their tentacle-covered neon faces. Their eyes are nothing but dark black orbs, with a small white circle on either one. They have no legs, and use fins and a tail to move around.
-Usual Height: 4-5 Feet Tall
-Usual Weight: 50-75 Pounds
-Danger Level: Extremely Low
-Place of Origin: Unknown
-Cross-Breed: No

• Canilupus

-Tall, Felishe-like creatures that have snout-like noses, tall floppy ears, and sharp fangs. Their bodies are covered in small hairs that are used to aid their complex touch sense. They're usually trained for combat from birth, and unlike Felishes, are not a cross-bred race.
-Usual Height: 6-7 Feet Tall
-Usual Weight: 135-155 Pounds
-Danger Level: Moderate
-Place of Origin: Canilue
-Cross-Breed: No

• Cobbles

-Creatures made from solid rock. Most of the time, they just take relaxing vacations on rock-heavy planets. They give GREAT hugs.
-Usual Height: 6-7 Feet Tall

-Usual Weight: 500-700 Pounds
-Danger Level: Low (When Not Disturbed)
-Place of Origin: Solidified Foremes
-Cross-Breed: No

• Creeschuns

-Tall necked, stubby bodied, nerds that excel in boring
people to death. They're usually librarians, tour guides, or
informational bodies. They traveled to Loca after their
home planet, Rhukers, was taken over by Trhools.
Dhamaneek was the last living Creeschun until Al-X took
his life during the Temple of Akur massacre.
-Usual Height: 8 Feet Tall
-Usual Weight: 50-145 Pounds
-Danger Level: Extremely Low
-Place of Origin: Rhukers
-Cross-Breed: Yes

• DemiGods

-Only seven demiGods actually exist. They were created to
hopefully stop the reign and fate of Magona. In some eyes,
they failed. In others, they still stopped Magona in one
way or another.
-Usual Height: Unknown
-Usual Weight: Unknown
-Danger Level: High
-Place of Origin: Meiv

-Cross-Breed: No

• Devil-Fetus

-The in-progress parasite to infect Al-X, taken too early, and resulted in the unkillable child of the Netherworld. An armless, soulless, motherless, baby that has a taste for spines.
-Usual Height: 2-3 Feet Tall
-Usual Weight: 20-35 Pounds
-Danger Level: Extremely High
-Place of Origin: Juwles
-Cross-Breed: No

• Dice Bots

-Al-X's casino guards; created from scraps left over from the Mechanical Carishem Revolution. Row-N hates the build of the Dice Bots, since they are very unstable and can't aid in anything but decoration. Al-X says Row-N is full of his own shit.
-Usual Height: 5-5.5 Feet Tall
-Usual Weight: 300-325 Pounds
-Danger Level: Low
-Place of Origin: Al-X
-Cross-Breed: No

• Dierariun

-Clumps of mud held together with the willpower of a singular heart-like creature. The being itself is the Dierariun, and the dirt around it acts as a makeshift bodysuit. They're cuddly, if you enjoy being dirty.
-Usual Height: 5 Feet Tall
-Usual Weight: 36-42 Pounds
-Danger Level: High
-Place of Origin: Dierary
-Cross-Breed: No

• Duhv

-Creatures that slightly resemble humans, and try to steal their identity all the time. Identity theft is not a joke. Unless there's a punchline to it.
-Usual Height: 6-7 Feet Tall
-Usual Weight: 120-150 Pounds
-Danger Level: Moderate
-Place of Origin: Darhvart
-Cross-Breed: No

• Felishe

-Furry humans with small noses, ears on the top of their heads, and eyes with thin pupils. Their hair can be any shade of brown, black, or white and they usually wear clothes that match it. Their eyes are sought after presents for little children on Inaz, since they are almost like a good luck charm. Felishes hate children, even their own, because of this.

-Usual Height: 7 Feet Tall

-Usual Weight: 115-120 Pounds

-Danger Level: Moderate

-Place of Origin: Earth II

-Cross-Breed: Yes

• Foremes

-Made from the gas of the Infinite Flames; a section of negative energy light years away that can create sentient, forever burning beings. They can take the parts of other beings in order to use them for themselves.

-Usual Height: 9-12 Feet Tall

-Usual Weight: 0 Pounds

-Danger Level: Extremely High

-Place of Origin: Infinite Flames

-Cross-Breed: No

• Formics

-Bug faced humans that usually cover their deformities with cloaks, hoods, and masks. They have large quantities of hair on their heads, which can come in any neon color. It matches their usually brightly colored skin, complete with silver eyes. Their bodies bulge with blood-heavy veins, and their mouths sit between two hairy pincers.

-Usual Height: 6-7 Feet Tall

-Usual Weight: 135-139 Pounds
-Danger Level: Moderately High
-Place of Origin: Formos
-Cross-Breed: Yes

• Humans

-Almost 97% of the time, humans are ranked among the worst possible species, the most boring, and the most likely to abuse your race. More people were happy then afraid when Earth II was destroyed, only because they thought it was the natural death of the planet. Humans are the main reason that Magona's plan exists, since they are the reason for most of the cross-bred species alive.
-Usual Height: 5-6 Feet Tall
-Usual Weight: 136 Pounds
-Danger Level: Non-existent
-Place of Origin: Earth I
-Cross-Breed: No

• Infrens

-Fiery beings that are the top cause of deforestation, house fires, and arson. Their hearts beat with the heat of 10,000°, which could boil someone's skin with a single touch. They're usually bright orange in color, and while most have been killed, some still roam the lands of beautiful worlds, wanting to turn it black and red.
-Usual Height: 5-6 Feet Tall

-Usual Weight: 150-175 Pounds
-Danger Level: High
-Place of Origin: The Netherworld
-Cross-Breed: No

• Kuroledies

-Beautiful beings that were the first species to be wiped out by Magona. There were only around 100 when he began his plan when he saw The Seventh fall in love with one. Now, The Seventh is haunted with the image of 100 graves dotting the barren Sarion grounds, and the memory of his Kuroledy taken from him.
-Usual Height: 4-6 Feet Tall
-Usual Weight: 75-100 Pounds
-Danger Level: Low
-Place of Origin: Sarion
-Cross-Breed: Yes

• Marajuanians

-Unbreakable wooden frames akin to a human skeleton, covered in grass and leaves. Their heart burns for eternity, and it burns the green, causing the surrounding people to sniff the fumes and can possibly go through psychedelic experiences. Ten out of ten scavengers recommend having a Marajuanian on your trip.
-Usual Height: 5.5-6 Feet Tall
-Usual Weight: 85-115 Pounds

-Danger Level: Extremely Low
-Place of Origin: Maraju
-Cross-Breed: No

• Mushrumians

-A native mushroom-headed species, coming from the lost planet of Mushrumia. They live in the caves of the samely-named Mushrumia, near the Province of Stoean's mining colony. Their bodies are usually featureless, white or gray blobs that they hop around on, and their heads are large mushroom tops with varying patterns. They do not have eyes, so they use vibrations to see, nor do they have mouths. They communicate only in the ancient Mushrumian language.
-Usual Height: 10 Feet Tall
-Usual Weight: 50-75 Pounds
-Danger Level: Extremely Low
-Place of Origin: Mushrumia (Planet)
-Cross-Breed: Yes

• Nag-Souls

-A silhouette of humans that is made of negative energy, which reverses gravity within its body. This causes the Nag-Souls to be a mirror of everything around it, but reflects everything in monotone, and in backwards order. Nag-Souls are used to show someone's future, but once seen, it cannot be changed. They are outlawed from entering any Cosmo-Edge ring planets.

-Usual Height: 5-6 Feet Tall

-Usual Weight: Reverses gravity inside its body

-Danger Level: High

-Place of Origin: Time

-Cross-Breed: No

• Orugnics

-Only a few Orugnics have been seen in the wild. Most decide to stay on their untouchable Cosmo-Edge ring planet of Orugno. Marz is one such traveler, and he represents the white-haired elders. Most Orugnics are fighters, trying to save their planet from the political corruption of the Treenun ring.

-Usual Height: 3-5 Feet Tall

-Usual Weight: 45-65 Pounds

-Danger Level: Moderately Low

-Place of Origin: Orugno

-Cross-Breed: Yes

• Phroug

-Tall, but bent creatures with an upside-down arch shape. Their legs connect at the top to the body, and large white eyes are embedded into their flesh. The feet are blocky stones that are compiled of bundled dead skin from

humans, usually. They're popular among billboard hangers, shooting ranges, and clubs, for some reason.
-Usual Height: 6 Feet Tall
-Usual Weight: 80-85 Pounds
-Danger Level: Moderate
-Place of Origin: Earth I
-Cross-Breed: Yes

• Pocomels

-Humans that traveled to Pocomel, and somehow evolved to become armless and legless. They must train with their upper body and mouth in order to create their own limbs. This causes most Pocomels to have chests as large as a doorframe, and a chin as sharp as a knife. They have since become one of the most intelligent races.
-Usual Height: 2-3 Feet Tall
-Usual Weight: 55-80 Pounds
-Danger Level: Low
-Place of Origin: Pocomel
-Cross-Breed: Yes

• Pēchaucks

-Elegant, stubby flyers with long necks, small heads, and skinny arms. Their legs are also slender, with four small toe-like bones poking out from the bottom. Their bodies are just circles decorated with colorful hairs that extrude with large feathers, acting as a symbol of their wisdom.

They are usually hated for being extremely annoying and hypocritical.

-Usual Height: 3-5 Feet Tall

-Usual Weight: 70-90 Pounds

-Danger Level: Low

-Place of Origin: Loca

-Cross-Breed: Yes

• Row-N's Leathean Machines

-The genius inventions from one Row-N. Machines built to help the construction of new towns and cities across Loca, and also aid in the findings of new medical practices. During the Magona takeover, Row-N perfected the body of his machines, but still stayed in his favorite model-A99 all his life.

-Usual Height: 8-10 Feet Tall

-Usual Weight: 1-2 Tons

-Danger Level: All

-Place of Origin: Row-N

-Cross-Breed: No

• The Divine

-Magona's original plan to start over. The Divine of every inhabited planet still remains, even Loca's. To the eye of mortals, The Divine is a ball of light akin to the sun. But to the view of DemiGods or those on the brink of death, its true appearance will be seen.

-Usual Height: Unknown
-Usual Weight: Unknown
-Danger Level: High
-Place of Origin: Magona
-Cross-Breed: No

• The Sacred

-The Divine's attempt to create a being that would scare away the population of a planet. After finding out that most species are worse than The Divine thought, it usually gave up and fell into a deep sleep. However, Loca's Sacred, Al-X, was subject to a lot of development as his own person, instead of being a puppet.
-Usual Height: Unknown
-Usual Weight: Unknown
-Danger Level: High
-Place of Origin: The Divine
-Cross-Breed: No

• Travish

-Buck tooth, big-eyed humans with dark colored skin. Their bodies are always moist, and they have large slits that connect to their lungs, allowing them to breathe above water. Their bodies are also decorated with tribal tattoos, since Travishes are very keen on keeping their roots close.
-Usual Height: 3-5 Feet Tall
-Usual Weight: 250-300 Pounds

-Danger Level: Low
-Place of Origin: Wastro
-Cross-Breed: Yes

• Treenuns

-Sentient trees that contain the same linked hivemind.
They are scary. They are approaching your location. Hide.
-Usual Height: 70-130 Feet Tall
-Usual Weight: 20,000-25,000 Pounds
-Danger Level: Unknown
-Place of Origin: Treenun
-Cross-Breed: No

• Varmpur

-A forest predator with sharp teeth and an unquenchable
thirst for blood. They usually have big builds, dark skin,
bald heads, and an unkillable smile that reveals their sharp
incisors. They usually hide in the tall Tranzle forests,
where they fall atop their prey. Despite their fierce
appearance, most do not know how to fight, and carry
floppy swords that appear like serrated steel ones.
-Usual Height: 6-7 Feet Tall
-Usual Weight: 150-200 Pounds
-Danger Level: Moderately High
-Place of Origin: Tranzle
-Cross-Breed: Yes

• Zargon

-Zargons are creatures that share similarities to most Earth II stories of dragons and reptiles. They have scales for skin, large horns on their heads, and an appetite for humans. All non-human species don't fear Zargons, but even beings with 1% human DNA are horrified when they see one. Zargons have the largest count for discrimination on Loca, and the highest amount of murders are of Zargons.

-Usual Height: 6-9 Feet Tall

-Usual Weight: 300-500 Pounds

-Danger Level: Dangerous

-Place of Origin: Zargo

-Cross-Breed: No

• Zhalk's Species

-Although most of this species is unknown, all that can be agreed upon is their five-armed bodies and creative clothing choices.

-Usual Height: Unknown

-Usual Weight: Unknown

-Danger Level: Unknown

-Place of Origin: Unknown

-Cross-Breed: Unknown

~The Order of The Universe~

● The Eternal Brain

-The very middle of the known universe and the center point for every universe that has and will ever exist. It binds all of time and space together and needs to be watched over.

-0 Planet Groups

-Currently Ungrouped Known Planets: The Eternal Brain

● Brain Ring

-The ring of planets that borders The Eternal Brain. A lot of smaller, more compact planets and civilizations. The most common religion amongst the inhabitants is a changed version of Sevrinchístt, where they believe The Eternal Brain to be their one true God.

-4 Planet Groups

-Currently Ungrouped Known Planets: Vecimt, Cöpar, Sarion, Mars II

● Mesial Ring

-Despite having fewer groups than the Churle Ring, the Mesial Ring is the most popular of them all. Roan used to be the most populated planet until the fall, and then Inaz took its spot until the Great Plummet of the economy, then Earth II took its spot until 2036, and now Loca is first for population.

-7 Planet Groups

-The Sol Planet Group: Mercury-X, Venus, Earth II, Mars III, Jupiter-Z, Saturn I, Uranus, Neptune-X, Pluto

-Currently Ungrouped Known Planets: Loca, Inaz, Roan, Mushrumia, Zargo, Secula

- ## Churle Ring

-The ring with the most, yet with the least. The Churle Ring has around 634 planets, yet only 4 of them are inhabitable. Most of the Churle Ring is clogged with Formes gasses that were left unchecked around the time Magona was banished.

-12 Planet Groups

-Currently Ungrouped Known Planets: Darhvart, Jouruesa, Formos, Maraju, Tranzle

- ## Astrual Ring

-The Astrual ring is the home of planets most people wish not to visit. The Valley is closed off to most, Earth I has a troubling history, and the other planets are just as suspicious.

-10 Planet Groups
-The Luna Planet Group: Earth I, Mars I, Saturn II, Neptune-Z
-Currently Ungrouped Known Planets: The Valley, Vhorlarx, Canilue, Shlurgant Supreme

• Hi-Tem Ring

-A ring of mostly washed up, tourist planets. The biggest hub for trading, hunting, gambling, and anything that groups can get together for. Also home to the universe's favorite refuel spot: Stalis Station.
-5 Planet Groups
-Stalis Planet Group: Stalis, Talvir
-Currently Ungrouped Known Planets: Rhukers, Pocomel, Shlurghant

• Cosmo-Edge Rings

-A ring that is made up of smaller rings of planets that borders the Cosmo barrier. Mostly advanced civilizations that have never traveled beyond the Hi-Tem ring.
-7 Rings, ~4 Planet Groups per Ring
-Known Rings:
–Fivtie Ring
–Known Fivtie Ring Planets: Beriackhayv, Crieyath, Orugno, Wastro

–Termehus Ring
–Known Termehus Ring Planets: Treenun
-Home To: The Infinite Flames, The Netherworld

• Cosmo Field

-A field that borders the universe of nothing. A void absent of anything, it even lacks nothingness. No explorer has dared to cross the Cosmo barrier, but maybe one day someone will.
-0 Planet Groups
-Currently Ungrouped Known Planets: 0